He'd be havin

Let's see how her ...
the next month.

Because he was going to give himself—and her—one month. One month of vengeance...

Three Rich Men

*Three Australian billionaires;
they can have anything and anyone...
except three beautiful women...*

Meet Charles, Rico and Ali,
three incredibly wealthy friends all living in
Sydney. They meet every Friday night to play
poker and exchange news about business and
their pleasures—which include the pursuit of
Sydney's most beautiful women.

Up until now, no woman has ever managed to
pin down any of these elusive, exclusive and
eminently eligible bachelors. But that's all about
to change. First Charles, then Rico and finally
Ali will fall for three gorgeous girls....

But will these three rich men marry for love—
or are they desired for their money?

A Rich Man's Revenge—Charles's story
#2349 October 2003

Mistress for a Month—Rico's story
#2361 December 2003

Sold to the Sheikh—Ali's story
#2374 February 2004

Miranda Lee

A RICH MAN'S REVENGE

Three Rich Men

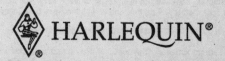

HARLEQUIN®

TORONTO • NEW YORK • LONDON
AMSTERDAM • PARIS • SYDNEY • HAMBURG
STOCKHOLM • ATHENS • TOKYO • MILAN • MADRID
PRAGUE • WARSAW • BUDAPEST • AUCKLAND

ISBN 0-373-12349-3

A RICH MAN'S REVENGE

First North American Publication 2003.

Visit us at www.eHarlequin.com

Printed in U.S.A.

CHAPTER ONE

"Do you have to play poker *every* Friday night, come rain, hail or shine?"

Charles glanced in the mirror at the reflection of the very beautiful blonde lying face down across his bed, her glorious golden hair spread out over her slender shoulders, her delicately pointed chin propped up in her hands. Her eyes, which were as big and blue as the sky, locked on to his, their expression beseeching.

Charles hesitated only slightly before continuing to button up his grey silk shirt. As much as the idea of joining her back on that bed was very tempting, his Friday-night poker game was non-negotiable.

"My poker buddies and I made a pact some time back," he explained. "If we're in Sydney on a Friday night, we have to show up. Actually, if we're in *Australia*, we have to show up. We can only cancel if we're overseas or in hospital. Although when Rico was in hospital after a skiing accident last winter, he insisted we all come and play in his room."

Charles smiled wryly to himself as he thought of his best friend and his mad passion for the game. "I suspect on the unlikely event of Rico marrying again he'd ask us to accompany him on the honeymoon, just to get his weekly fix. I, however, was more than happy to give up poker during the entire month of *my* honeymoon," he pointed out rather smugly.

"Your wife would have been seriously displeased if you hadn't."

"Would she?" He turned and smiled down at her. "How displeased?"

"*Very* displeased."

"And are you displeased tonight, Mrs Brandon?"

She shrugged; then rolled over onto her back, stretching languorously against the ivory satin sheets, her hands lifting up over her head to flop against the side of the king-sized bed. Charles tried not to look at her simply perfect body. But it was difficult not to wallow in her physical beauty. Dominique was every man's fantasy come true. And she was all his.

Charles still could not believe his luck in winning the hand—and the love—of such a glorious creature.

And Dominique *did* love him. He'd dated enough fortune hunters in the past to know the real thing when he found it.

Dominique sighed as she glanced up at him through her long lashes. "I suppose I can spare you for a few hours. I'm going to have to get used to being by myself, anyway, since you're going back to work next Monday."

Back to work...

Charles groaned at the thought, which was a first. For the past twenty years he'd devoted his life to the family brewery business after it had been brought to the brink of bankruptcy by his profligate father. And he'd loved every difficult, challenging, frustrating moment.

From the age of twenty to forty he'd lived and breathed Brandon Beer. Marriage and a family had been relegated to the back-burner as he'd gone from being a near penniless undergraduate to one of Australia's most successful businessmen, putting Brandon Beer back on the world map and buying half a dozen Sydney hotels along the way, each of which now earned him a sizeable fortune from the recent addition of poker machines.

Since meeting and marrying Dominique, however, business had taken a back seat in Charles's life. His mind had been focused on things other than investment opportunities, market projections and expansion programmes. Even now, with the honeymoon over, his focus remained on things other than work.

The prospect of starting a family in the near future excited him almost as much as did the woman he planned having that family with. Dominique wanted at least two children and had decided to stop taking the Pill next month, which pleased him no end, as did her decision not to go back to work herself after their honeymoon. She'd quit her job in the PR department at Brandon Beer's head office shortly after she'd said yes to his proposal, saying she didn't feel right, working there any more.

Charles was well aware, however, that with her looks and personality Dominique could secure another PR or PA job in Sydney at the drop of a hat. And he'd said as much, not wanting her to think he was the kind of chauvinistic husband who expected his wife not to work.

But she'd said no to that suggestion, stating that for the next few years her career was being his wife, and the mother of his children. Maybe, when their last child went off to school, she would consider returning to the workforce.

Whilst not believing himself an old-fashioned man in any way, Charles had to confess he liked the thought of his wife always being there for him when he got home from work, ready to accommodate his every wish and whim, something which didn't seem to be any hardship for her.

"I'm going to miss you terribly," she said somewhat plaintively. "Are you quite sure you have to go back to work on Monday?" she asked, then gave him one of the best come-hither looks since Eve flashed that apple at Adam.

Charles's flesh responded accordingly. He didn't doubt he could survive being away from Dominique for a few hours this evening, but the prospect of not being able to make love to her during the day whenever he felt like it in future was not to his liking. Honeymoons were obviously very corrupting, as were beautiful brides who never said no to whatever their husbands wanted to do.

"I suppose I could take another week off," he said, thinking to himself that the office would survive another five days without his making a personal appearance. He could keep in touch by phone and email. "It would give us some time to look for our new house together." He'd told Dominique to look around for a real home to replace his present penthouse pad, something substantial and stylish in one of the Eastern suburbs. He didn't want to negotiate the harbour bridge on his way to the office every day.

Dominique beamed at him. "What a wonderful idea! But would you really? Take another week off work, I mean? I know your reputation for being a workaholic."

His eyes were rueful as they met Dominique's in the mirror. "You know I'd do just about anything you asked me to." Anything except give up any more of his Friday-night poker games.

His shirt safely buttoned, he turned and braced himself on the mattress on either side of her upside down face. "But you already know that, don't you?" he murmured, his mouth hovering just above hers. "You've bewitched me good and proper."

"Have I?" Her voice went all soft and smoky in that way which always turned him on. Charles groaned. It was incredible, really, given he was nearly forty-one years old, not some young buck in his prime. His desire for Dominique sometimes bordered on insatiable. Charles had never known a woman like her. Or a love like the love he felt for her. It was all-consuming. Possessive. Obsessive, even.

Her hands lifted to touch him, her eyebrows arching. "Mmm. Charles darling, I can't see you concentrating on cards in such a deplorable condition. Surely your poker buddies wouldn't mind if you were just a teensie weensie bit late…"

He ached to give in to her. But feared that once she started on him, he wouldn't want to stop. If he didn't show up at poker tonight, Rico would have his hide.

No. He'd have to be strong and not let Dominique have her wicked way with him this once.

Which perhaps was just as well. Always getting your own way was never good for anyone, but especially a wife, he imagined. He'd already spoiled Dominique shockingly since she'd become Mrs Charles Brandon. He'd spent a small fortune on designer fashion during their fortnight in Paris. And quite a bit on Italian handmade shoes and other accessories during their stopover in Rome.

But enough was enough. Now that their honeymoon was technically over, he really had to start the day-to-day routine of his marriage as he meant to go on. And he meant to go on playing poker every Friday night.

"On the contrary, my sweet," Charles said with a wry smile as he pulled back out of her reach. "Redirected sexual energies can be very effective. Frustration gives a man an edge. That's why boxers abstain the night before they fight. I guarantee I'll win at the table tonight, and when I finally get home so will you, my love. Now, do stop trying to seduce me, wench. Cover yourself up with a sheet or something till I can get myself out of here. That body of yours should be registered as a lethal weapon.''

She laughed, and rolled over onto her front again. ''Will that do?''

''Better, I guess.'' Though goodness knew her rear view was almost as tantalising as her front. He loved the way her spine curved down her long, slender back, dipping in at her tiny waist before rising to disappear between her peach-shaped behind. Like the rest of her, there was nothing even remotely boyish about Dominique's bottom. It was lush and pouty and perfect. A temptation of the most devilish kind.

Charles knew he wasn't the sort of man most women lusted after on sight. Never had been. As a teenager, girls hadn't looked at him twice. He hadn't fared much better as a young man. Of course, once he became seriously rich it was amazing how many gorgeous girls suddenly found him irresistible. But whilst his looks had improved considerably with age, one could still never call him handsome. Not in the way his father had been handsome. Or Rico. They were both movie-star material. So, Charles had often suspected some of his lady-friends had an eye on his money, rather than being genuinely attached or attracted to him.

Yes, the mirror told Charles the truth when he shaved every morning. He was now a passably attractive man, his main physical assets being his height, his fitness and that inherited gene which meant he'd never lose his full head of thick dark brown hair.

Baldness did not run in the Brandon family.

Of course, Charles had to concede that his successes in life had leant a certain air to the way he conducted himself nowadays. Some financial journalists described him as impressive and imposing. Others inclined towards ruthless and arrogant.

He didn't care what they wrote and said about him, really. Or even what the mirror told him. All that mattered was what Dominique saw when she looked at him.

Clearly, she found him attractive enough. *Very* attractive, actually. She'd confessed to him on their wedding night that her first emotion on meeting him was worry over how incredibly sexy she found him.

Charles could still remember the intense emotion which consumed *him* when he had first come face to face with his future wife. Rico had insisted it was just lust, but Charles knew differently. He knew he'd fallen in love at first sight.

The occasion was the company Christmas party last year, barely five months ago. Dominique had just started work at Brandon Beer that week after moving to Sydney from Melbourne. They hadn't met prior to the party, though he'd been aware of her appointment to their PR division. He'd seen—and approved—her CV.

He knew she was twenty-eight years old, a Tasmanian by birth, with no fancy education or degree to her credit, but a string of night-school diplomas which showed the sort of hard work and drive he admired. Her previous position in Melbourne had been with a sports and entertainment management company, her first job as a personal PA. To the boss of the place, no less. She'd been with him over two years and the reference he'd supplied was glowing. Prior to that she'd worked in reception and guest relations at some quality Melbourne hotels, a step up from her first job of being a housemaid.

Charles had been informed by the man who'd hired her that she was a very good-looking blonde, but seeing Ms Dominique Cooper in the flesh had literally taken his breath away.

She'd been wearing white, he recalled. A calf-length dress with a deep V-neckline which displayed her fabulous figure. Her hair had been up, tiny tendrils kissing her elegantly long neck. Her full lips had been shiny and pink. Pearl drops had dangled from her ears. When he drew closer, his nostrils had been filled with her perfume, an exotic and provocative scent which he now knew was called Casablanca.

He'd asked her out within minutes of being introduced, his desire already at fever pitch. Charles was used to getting his own way with women by then, so he'd been shocked by her refusal, especially when she admitted on further questioning that she wasn't seeing anyone else at the time. She'd told him politely but firmly that she would never date her boss, no matter how attractive she thought he was.

"So you do think I'm attractive," he countered, flattered yet frustrated at the same time.

She gave him an oddly nervous look, whirled on her high heels and fled the party.

Smitten and intrigued, he pursued her doggedly over the Christmas and New Year break, ringing her at home every evening and sending flowers to her flat every day—her number and address were in the personnel files at work—till she finally agreed to a dinner date. She still insisted he meet her at the restaurant rather than pick her up. She did not want him taking her home afterwards, which intrigued him further. Clearly, she was afraid to be alone with him. Why?

He didn't find out why till dessert, when she'd explained with quite touching agitation that she'd been foolish enough to date her last boss, then been even more foolish in becoming his secret mistress. He'd promised her the world, but in the end had dumped her and married some society girl with the right connections. That was why she'd moved to Sydney, to get right away from the awful memories, at the same time deciding that she would never again date her boss. Such men could not be trusted. They used silly girls like her because they were pretty and easily impressed. But they didn't love them, or marry them. They just screwed them, and screwed up their lives.

Charles set out to prove her wrong, but she was very difficult to convince. She did accept further·invitations to dinner with him and showed him in many incredibly sweet ways that she liked him a lot, but she continued to spurn any advances. Charles became even more enamoured, and vowed to show her that his feelings for her were above board.

He could still remember the look on her face when he told her over dinner one night in early March that he loved her more than words could say. But when he asked her to marry him, producing the most beautiful—and the most expensive—diamond ring he'd been able to buy, her shock quickly turned to disgust.

"You don't mean that," she retorted. "You're just saying it to get me into bed. You think you can buy my love, but you've wasted your money on that rock because the pathetic truth is I've *already* fallen in love with you. I was going to go to bed with you tonight, anyway."

He wasn't able to contain his delight at this announcement. *Or* his desire. He'd never been so hard.

"Oh, just put the rotten thing on my finger if it makes you feel better," she swept on irritably. "Then take me to wherever it is you have in mind to take me. But you and I both know you won't go through with any wedding. After you've had what you want, you'll dump me like my last boss."

"You're wrong," he insisted passionately as he slipped the sparkling rock on her engagement finger.

And he proved her wrong by marrying her a month later without having so much as laid a finger on her. The kiss he gave her after their very small and unostentatious ceremony was their first proper kiss. It had been sheer and utter hell to control himself for so long but he'd managed by focusing on the big picture.

Rico called him insane, marrying a woman he hadn't been intimate with before. A strange sentiment for a man of Italian heritage. Weren't they into virgin brides? Not that Dominique was a virgin. She'd never pretended to be.

But there was a touchingly virginal air about her when she came to him on their wedding night, trembling in her white satin nightgown. Clearly, she was nervous, afraid perhaps that she'd made a big mistake herself, marrying a man *she'd* never been intimate with. For all she knew he could have been the worst lover in the world!

But their wedding night was magic for both of them. Sheer magic. When he witnessed his new bride's awed joy, his own pleasure and satisfaction was boundless.

"I didn't know what real love was till this moment," Dominique had told him as she lay still snuggled up to him somewhere close to dawn. "I love you so much, Charles. I'd die if you ever stopped loving me back."

Impossible, he'd thought at the time. And he still thought the same. If anything, he was more in love with her than ever. *He'd* be the one who'd die if *she* ever stopped loving *him*.

"I have to go," he told her gently, feeling slightly guilty for leaving her alone now. "I'll try not to stay too late, but—"

"Yes, I know," she broke in with a sigh. "I understand. Rico will try to keep you there till all hours."

Dominique clenched her teeth at the thought of Charles's best man doing just that. And it had nothing to do with Rico being a poker addict.

Enrico Mandretti's scepticism over her love for Charles had been evident from their first meeting. Clearly, he thought her a devious fortune hunter. He didn't have to spell out his suspicions. They were there in his dark, cynical eyes.

The trouble was…he was right. Yet oh, so wrong.

She *did* love Charles. More than she'd ever thought herself capable of loving any man. But before she'd met her future husband she'd been exactly what Rico believed she was. A gold-digger. A good-looking girl using her looks and her body to achieve her main goal in life: to acquire a wealthy husband, a gold-plated insurance policy that she would never have to suffer what her mother had suffered.

Dominique was sure that rich men's wives didn't go through what her mother had gone through. They were protected from such ignominies. They could at least die with dignity. That was, if they had to die at *all*.

After her mother's lingering and very painful death, Dominique had vowed that she would marry money, if it was the last thing she did. Becoming a rich man's wife, however, proved not such an easy task, not even for a girl with *her* looks. Rich men married women who moved in their own social circles. Or girls who worked with them; sophisticated, educated creatures with university degrees.

Unfortunately, Dominique's education had been sadly lacking during her teenage years, her schooling constantly interrupted then totally terminated so that she could stay home and nurse her mother till she passed away. By the time she was eighteen, Dominique knew it would take years before she had the skills which would put her into the immediate vicinity of wealthy businessmen.

But she had youth on her side, and tenacity, and she'd finally achieved her aim a couple of years back, that of being in the right place, working alongside the right kind of boss. Single. Good-looking. And rich.

Unfortunately, her target had been even more ruthless than she was. *His* life's plan did not include getting hitched to some no-account girl from the backwoods of Tasmania, no matter how hard she'd worked to educate herself, or how much he fancied her.

Sleeping with her was fine. Lying to her perfectly OK. Marrying her? Never in a million years!

After her mission to become Mrs Jonathon Hall had failed, a distressed and a slightly bitter Dominique had taken her over-generous severance pay along with Jonathon's guilt-ridden, glowing reference and headed for the bigger fish pond of Sydney. Once there, she'd plotted out her strategy for becoming Mrs

Charles Brandon with cold-blooded resolve. More cold-blooded than ever.

But there had been nothing cold-blooded about the feelings Charles had evoked in her during their first meeting. She'd already seen photographs of him and thought him quite attractive—Dominique knew she couldn't bear to marry a man who was physically repulsive to her—but she'd found Charles in the flesh so intensely sexy she'd been totally thrown.

Those icy grey eyes of his had cut right through her defences to that part of her which she'd kept locked tightly away all her life. Dominique had never fallen in love before. Or even into lust. She had felt varying degrees of attraction to members of the opposite sex over the years. She'd even slept with a few. Jonathon, she'd been *very* attracted to. Sex with him had been quite pleasurable, but she'd never been carried away by it, or really needed it. Oh, no. All her responses with Jonathon had been totally faked.

Yet when Charles had stared at her body none too subtly that first day, she'd found herself staring right back at his own tall, lean body and wanting it so very badly.

Panic best described her reaction to this alien craving. It was no wonder she had fled, totally abandoning her plan to seduce Charles Brandon. She wanted to *marry* a rich man, not fall in love with one. Love made a woman weak and foolish and vulnerable. Love brought misery, not happiness.

But Charles wouldn't leave it at that, would he?

And here she was, his wife; his adoring and besotted wife.

Now she knew what her mother had meant when Dominique had once asked her why she'd married a man like her wretched father.

"Because I loved him to death," had been her mother's reply.

Words of considerable irony.

As Dominique watched her husband put on his jacket, she tried not to worry about loving him so deeply. She supposed that with Charles she could afford to be a little weak and foolish and vulnerable. Because he loved her back. And he wasn't anything like Jonathon.

How perverse, she thought, that she'd targeted Charles for that very reason. Because he wasn't as young or as handsome as Jonathon. She'd thought that would make Charles more susceptible to seduction. She'd thought that would give her more power over him.

But just the opposite had happened. He'd been the one who'd exercised all the power over her, coercing her to go out with him, despite her fear of falling for him.

Yet she *was* happy, wasn't she? Deliriously so. There was nothing to be afraid of. Charles was a wonderful husband and lover. And he'd make a wonderful father.

That was another thing which constantly surprised Dominique. Her desire now for children. She'd never thought of herself as maternal before. Never wanted to be the little woman at home. Now she simply couldn't wait to have a baby with Charles. Not just one, either. Suddenly, her idea of Utopia was being his little woman at home with the patter of little feet around her.

Of course, her home would be nothing like her mother's home. Not a shack, but a mansion. *Her* husband was a man of substance who could provide in abundance for his wife and any number of children, not some pathetic failure of a man who couldn't even look after himself, let alone anyone else.

"I'm off now," Charles said as he swept up his cellphone and car keys from the bedside chest. "You know my number if you need me. Be good, now…" And he threw her a wry smile.

A premonition-type panic gripped her heart as she watched him walk towards the bedroom door.

"Charles!" she called out, and he turned, frowning.

"What is it?"

"Nothing. I…I love you."

"I know," he said, smiling again, a little smugly this time. "Keep it warm for me." And he left.

CHAPTER TWO

THE distance between Charles's inner-city apartment block and the Regency Hotel was only a couple of blocks, but Charles still drove. Walking was not his favourite form of exercise. Within five minutes of leaving Dominique, Charles was handing the keys of his silver Jaguar car to the parking attendant at the Regency and striding inside the five-star hotel.

Hurrying across the marble floor, he was passing the row of trendy and exclusive boutiques which lined the spacious arcade-style foyer when his eyes landed on a spectacular piece of jewelry, displayed under a spotlight in the window of Whitmores Opals. Charles ground to a halt and stared at the magnificent choker necklace which was made of two rows of oval-shaped milk opals surrounded by diamonds and linked together with finely filigreed gold.

How marvellous it would look on Dominique with her long, elegant neck and fair hair!

A glance at his watch showed it wasn't yet eight. He had twelve minutes before he was officially late. The shop was still open. These shops remained open till nine every Friday night.

The price was steep, of course. Quality jewels didn't come cheap. He tried telling himself that he really had to stop spoiling Dominique like this, but it was too late. He could already see her wearing it.

The decision made, Charles strode inside and five minutes later he had the necklace in his jacket pocket, nestled in a classy black leather box lined with thick black velvet. By the time he'd collected his visitor's pass-key from Reception and ridden the private lift up to the top floor, it was two minutes to eight. He still had a minute to spare as the lift doors whooshed back and the door to the presidential suite lay straight ahead.

When he'd first told Dominique where he played poker on a Friday night, she'd queried the choice of such an expensive venue. Why didn't they just go to each other's homes? So much cheaper.

He'd explained that it was of no cost to him. One of his poker buddies was an Arab sheikh who stayed in the Regency's top suite every weekend, flying in by helicopter every Friday afternoon from his Hunter Valley property.

Naturally, Dominique had been agog at this news and wanted to know more about this mysterious sheikh who played poker with her husband. Charles had told her the scant details he knew, which was that Prince Ali was thirty-three years old, sinfully handsome and the youngest son of King Khaled of Dubar, one of the wealthiest Emirate states. With four older brothers, Ali was unlikely to ever ascend the throne and had been despatched to Australia several years ago, ostensibly to take care of the royal family's race-horse interests here.

And he'd certainly done a good job of that. The royal thoroughbred stud boasted some of the top-priced yearlings at the Easter sales every year. Rumour had it, however, that Ali's skills as a horseman and businessman had nothing to do with his selection for his present position as manager of the royal stud. Apparently, he'd been exiled from Dubar for his own personal safety after some scandal involving a married woman.

Probably true, in Charles's opinion. Ali had gathered a reputation for being a ladies' man in Australia as well, though not in any obvious man-about-town way. He was never seen out in public alone with a woman, or photographed with one. Word was when he met a good-looking girl who took his eye during his weekly visits to the races in Sydney, private arrangements were made, and if the object of his desire was willing she was whisked up to his country property.

None of Ali's so-called girlfriends had ever sold their story to the media, so, really, talk of these liaisons was all speculation and gossip. Ali never personally revealed anything about his love life, being a very private man.

Charles suspected, however, that this gossip was probably true, too. A man of Ali's extraordinary wealth and looks would find it almost impossible not to become a playboy in the bedroom department.

He'd been a bit of a one himself before he'd met Dominique. Yet he wasn't in Ali's league. The man was a prince, for heaven's sake.

Ali's royal status was the reason they played in his suite here every Friday night, rather than have him visit them. Everything was more secure and more relaxed that way. On the occasion they'd gone to Rico's hospital room last year, Ali had been accompanied by two hired bodyguards. One had stood outside the hospital-room door all night whilst the other had sat in a corner of the room, *after* he'd drawn the shades on the window.

A bit unsettling.

In the hotel suite, there was no need for that. Hotel security was always on high alert when Prince Ali was in residence and no one could access the presidential suite without a pass-key for the lift. Even then, their identity was fully checked out a second time via camera during the ride up in the private lift, and again at the door to the presidential suite.

Charles lifted his hand to ring the doorbell, the door being whisked open within seconds. Clearly, his arrival had been anticipated.

"Good evening, Mr Brandon," the butler greeted.

"It certainly is, James," Charles replied as he walked in. "Very good."

"I trust you had an enjoyable honeymoon, sir," the butler went on in his usual formal manner. Charles suspected he'd been to a school for butlers in England.

Somewhere in his late thirties, tall and dignified-looking with a patrician nose and close-cut sandy blond hair, James was the house butler assigned to the presidential suite at the Regency every Friday night. He was always polite and respectful, and his attention to detail was incredible, as was his memory for names and faces and facts.

"It was marvellous," Charles replied. "Paris in the spring is always superb."

"And Mrs Brandon?"

Charles grinned. "She's superb, too."

James allowed himself a small smile. "If I may say so, sir, you're looking extra well."

"I'm feeling extra well."

"I can't say the same for Mr Mandretti," he murmured, his voice dropping to a low, conspiratorial tone.

"Oh? Has Rico been ill whilst I've been away?" Charles knew that the trio would have still continued to play poker here every Friday night, calling up a substitute player.

"No, not physically ill. I think he has something on his mind. He's been quite short with me tonight, and that's not like Mr Mandretti at all."

No, it wasn't. A self-made success story, Rico was inclined to treat the workers in this world much more politely than the privileged people he now mixed with. He liked and admired Charles because he'd earned his money through hard work and not just inheritance. Rico had little respect for the silver-spooned species.

An exception was their host every Friday night.

Prince Ali might have had his fortune bestowed on him through birth, being one of the pampered sons of an oil-rich Arab sheikh. But he was no sloth. Apparently, he worked his royal backside off at that stud farm he ran, very much a hands-on man when it came to his beloved horses.

Rico had stayed at Ali's property a few times, and seen the man in action for himself. He thought Ali an OK guy, despite his billions, and treated him accordingly.

On the other hand, the fourth and last member of their private poker club wasn't the recipient of Rico's total respect. Rico obviously had ambivalent feelings towards Mrs Renée Selinsky. Although Renée had been very working class before making it big, first as a model, then as the owner of a highly successful modelling agency, Rico had difficulty overlooking the fact she'd subsequently married a banker old enough to be her grandfather.

In his eyes, marrying for money—Rico couldn't conceive that she might have actually *loved* a man in his sixties—was just as bad as inheriting it.

By thirty, Renée had become an extremely rich widow, and had started buying shares in racehorse syndicates. That was how the four of them had met, because they'd all bought shares in one of Ali's beautifully bred yearlings.

On the day their colt had run in and won the Silver Slipper Stakes, the three celebrating owners—and one very proud breeder—had discovered a mutual love of poker. The four of them had played their first game that Saturday night in this very suite.

That had been around five years ago. Now the merry widow, as Rico sometimes called Renée, was thirty-five, still a looker, and still possessing that cool, self-contained air which seemed to get under Rico's skin.

But it was her brilliant brain which niggled Rico the most. He hated it when she beat him at poker. But Renée's bluffing was sometimes simply superb and totally unpredictable. None of them could match her when she was on her game.

Charles accepted her superiority on those occasions with pragmatic logic and played conservatively, hating to waste his money. Ali often tried to force her to fold by raising the stakes outrageously high, and was sometimes successful. Renée was rich, but not in Ali's league. Rico, however, would become testy and rude, sniping at her in a vain attempt to break her nerve, then inevitably making the wrong call, folding when he should have stayed in, and raising when she had an unbeatable hand.

Privately, Charles suspected that Rico fancied the merry widow but wouldn't admit it, even to himself. There was something decidedly sexual in his eyes when he delivered his barbs on these occasions.

There again, Rico was an extremely sexual animal.

At thirty-four, he was still in his prime, a Latin-lover type brimming with testosterone and over-the-top passions.

Charles wondered if Rico's rudeness to the butler tonight had something to do with an overload of male hormones. He'd been divorced over a year now and there wasn't any permanent replacement in his bed as yet. Which was not right for Rico. He was a man who needed to make love, often!

Some warm womanly love wouldn't go astray, ei--ther.

Charles believed Rico needed a wife, someone who loved him this time, someone like his Dominique who wanted children. But Rico wasn't about to go down the aisle again in a hurry. Once bitten, he wasn't shy so much as angry, angry that he'd been taken in by a gold-digger.

The appearance of the man himself in the archway which led into the main sitting room showed Charles that James had the situation spot-on. Rico wasn't in any way ill. He looked his usual swashbuckling self in black trousers and a black crewnecked top, his thick, wavy black hair as lustrous as ever, his flashing black eyes as clear as a bell. But he was definitely out of sorts, scowling as he quaffed back the last of the drink he was holding. It looked like Chianti. Rico loved his Italian wines, despite having been born here, in Sydney.

"About bloody time you got here," he snapped without a trace of the Italian accent he adopted for his popular *A Passion for Pasta* TV show. His parents had migrated to Sydney over half a century earlier, not long after the Second World War; all their eight children had been born here—three boys and five girls—and Rico was the youngest.

Charles couldn't get his head around the idea of so many siblings. He didn't have any.

"I'm right on time," Charles countered calmly, in far too good a mood to be riled by Rico's burst of Latin temper.

"No, you're not. The game is supposed to be underway by eight. It's already five minutes past, courtesy of your gasbagging and gossiping out here with the hired help. Here, James, fill this up again, will you?" Rico said curtly and handed the butler his empty glass.

Charles wondered what was eating at Rico but he decided not to ask. Best to just get in there and start playing poker.

The others were already sitting at the card table where it was always set up, next to the bullet-proof plate-glass window which overlooked the city below. Renée, looking softer than usual in a pale pink cashmere sweater, lifted her glass of white wine in Charles's direction in acknowledgement of his arrival.

Ali, dressed in blue jeans and a shirt, managed a polite nod as he sipped his usual glass of mineral water. Ali never touched alcohol himself but always supplied the best in spirits and wine for his guests.

"See, Rico?" Renée said in that silky voice of hers

as the two men sat down at the table. "I told you he'd show up. Though he'd be forgiven if he didn't. After all, he's only been married to that stunner of a wife of his for a month."

Renée was still a stunner herself, Charles appreciated. Just not his type. Too tall and too thin. And a brunette. Charles preferred blondes, and a softer more feminine kind of beauty.

There was nothing soft about Renée. But she was very striking, with those high cheekbones and unusual eyes. Pale green they were, with rather heavy lids which she emphasised by plucking her eyebrows to the finest of arches. The set of her eyebrows gave her face a range of expressions, none of which were soft or sweet. When smiling, she looked either drily amused or downright sardonic. Unsmiling, Renée carried an air about her which could be interpreted as snobbishness, or at the very least belief in her own superiority. Possibly this had been an asset on the catwalk, where models specialised in looking aloof these days. But not such an asset in one's social life.

Charles had not liked her to begin with. But first impressions were not always correct, he'd found. He still could not claim to know her all that well, even now after five years' acquaintance. But he'd warmed to her after a while. Impossible to totally dislike a woman who could play poker as well as she did, and who had what he called strength of character. Renée was always her own person, and he admired that.

It didn't matter to him if she'd married the banker

for his money or not. No doubt she had her reasons. Still, Renée was far too cool and controlled for him. Not like Dominique, who was a wonderful mixture of sweet surrender and wildly impassioned demands.

"Again, Charles," she'd beg him, even after he thought he was done. But he was rarely ever done with Dominique.

Damn. He shouldn't have started thinking about Dominique.

After they had cut cards for the deal—which Renée won, much to Rico's irritation—Charles tried to settle back to enjoy the game. But it was no use. His concentration was shot to pieces. By the time they broke off for supper at ten-thirty, he was losing more than he liked.

"Your mind's not on your game tonight, Charles," Ali remarked over coffee and cake.

"I'm just a bit rusty," he replied.

"Maybe he's setting us all up for a sting later on in the evening," Renée suggested.

Charles smiled what he hoped was an enigmatic smile.

"Trust you to think that," Rico snapped. "That's just the sort of thing a devious female like you would do. But Charles is a straight shooter. The reason he's not playing well tonight is because he can't keep his thoughts above his waist."

"And who could blame him?" Ali said in that rich Eton-educated voice of his. "Renée is right. You are a very lucky man, Charles, to have found a woman so beautiful for your bed.''

Charles bristled at the inference that Dominique's role in his life was nothing more than sexual.

''Dominique has a beautiful mind as well as a beautiful body, Ali,'' he said with a hint of reproach in his voice. ''We are friends as well as lovers. Equals, in every way.''

Rico laughed. ''Who do you think you're kidding, Charles? That girl has you by the short and curlies.''

''Must you be so crude?'' Renée said with a withering glance Rico's way. ''Take no notice of him, Charles. He's just jealous because he can't find anyone to love, or who truly loves him in return.''

Rico laughed again, yet it had a hard, hollow ring to it. ''I wish I were jealous. Oh, yes. That would be much better.''

''Better than what?'' Charles asked, not quite following Rico's train of thought.

Rico looked remorseful for opening his mouth. ''Nothing. I'm rambling. I've had too much to drink. I think I'll stick to coffee for the rest of the night.''

''An excellent idea, Enrico,'' Ali said. ''Alcohol is the root of all evil.''

''I thought that was money,'' Rico retorted.

''No. It's sex,'' Renée surprised them all by saying. ''Sex is the root of all evil. We would all be much better off without it.''

''But then there wouldn't be any children,'' Charles pointed out.

"Exactly," she returned.

"Trust you not to like children," came Rico's cutting comment.

Renée stiffened. "I didn't say that. But the world is overpopulated as it is. And so many children are suffering. I would rather there be no more children than to see such suffering."

"Sorry, but I can't oblige you there, Renée," Charles piped up. "Dominique and I are planning to have children. And soon."

Rico's eyes jerked his way. "I thought you'd put that off for a while," he said with a frown. "Hell, Charles, you've only been married a month!"

"I'm forty-one next birthday, Rico. I haven't got time to waste. Besides, Dominique's keen to have a baby."

"Is she, now?" he said, and Charles heard the cynical note which always flavoured Rico's voice when he spoke about Dominique.

Rico didn't like Dominique. Charles could no longer ignore that fact. Why Rico didn't like her was just as obvious. He thought Dominique was a gold-digger, like his own ex.

Charles could have been insulted by his friend's opinion—didn't he think any woman could love him for himself?—but he understood Rico was still going through a bitter phase after his own wretched marital experience. In time, he'd realise Dominique wasn't anything like Jasmine. When that happened he might even decide to give marriage another go himself.

''I think we should cease to discuss personal issues and get back to the game,'' Ali suggested wisely. ''That is why we meet here each Friday night. To play poker and to escape life's little stresses and strains for a while. Let us leave such matters at the door in future.''

Rico and Renée both gave Ali a look which implied a man of his massive power and privilege wasn't subjected to too many of life's little stresses and strains.

Till Charles had met Dominique, he might have agreed with them. Money and success had certainly smoothed his path in life. But he knew now that it didn't bring real happiness. Love did.

Without love, having all the money in the world could become very empty indeed. Charles suspected Ali was no more happy in his private life than was Rico, or the merry widow. You only had to look into that woman's eyes to know *she* wasn't happy. Not where it mattered. Not in her heart.

Earlier, she'd made it sound as if she didn't want children. But was that the truth? Or was it a rationalisation of where her life was heading, fast past that age where it was easy for a woman to conceive, especially without a partner?

Charles was only guessing, of course. Renée was like Ali, never revealing much about her private life. Presumably she did have a love life, but what kind and with whom Charles had no idea. All he knew was that she always showed up at the races alone. And she never cancelled on a Friday night. Unusual for a woman.

There again, Renée was an unusual woman. An enigma. A rather intimidating enigma. Charles pitied any man who ever fell in love with her. No man wanted to be intimidated by his woman. They wanted a woman who could make a man feel good about himself, the way Dominique did.

Aah…Dominique. She was very much on his mind tonight. Ali could command they leave their personal lives at the door but Charles couldn't do that just yet. His love for his lovely wife was all too new, and all too consuming.

He patted the jewelry box in his jacket pocket before he sat back down again, his stomach tightening in pleasurable anticipation of that moment when she opened the lid and saw the necklace. He couldn't wait to put it on her, to see how it looked.

The next two hours dragged, his play deteriorating further. Ali shook his head at his many mistakes. Renée smiled wryly and Rico scowled.

"What am I going to do with you, Charles?" Rico said when the night's poker was over and the two men rode the lift together down to the ground floor. Renée had already gone ahead, always the first to leave after play was halted, usually around midnight. Tonight it had been twelve-thirty, due to their late start.

Charles laughed. "I'll do better next week," he said, thinking that by then he might have the worst of his lust out of his system.

Not that he said that to Rico. Rico would pounce on the word lust, and claim he'd been right all along; it was just the promise of sex which had bewitched and entrapped him.

But Charles knew that wasn't the case. It was only natural that he and Dominique were still going through that phase when they couldn't keep their hands off each other. Unlike most newlyweds these days, they hadn't been living together before their wedding. Hell, they hadn't even kissed!

"Did you mean it when you said you and Dominique weren't waiting to have children?"

Rico's question surprised Charles. "Why would I lie about something like that?"

"But you haven't actually gotten her pregnant yet."

"No. She's on the Pill for now. But she's coming off it next month."

"I honestly don't think that's a good idea, Charles. You should wait at least a year before you take such a big step. Get to know your wife a bit better first. You hardly know the girl, after all."

Charles's forbearance over Rico's negative attitude towards Dominique began to wane. "I know all I need to know," he replied tautly. "Look, Rico, I realise you don't like Dominique. You probably think she's a fortune hunter, but—"

"You're wrong," Rico interrupted, his expression grim. "I don't *think* she's a fortune hunter, my friend. I *know* she's a fortune hunter."

CHAPTER THREE

CHARLES whirled, his fists balling by his sides. "Now, look here, Rico, I'm warning you. Stop this once and for all. Just because Jasmine took you for a ride, doesn't mean that Dominique's doing the same to me. My wife loves me. Renée's right. You're jealous."

The lift doors opened on the ground floor and Charles gave Rico one last uncompromising glare. "I suggest you apologise before we leave this lift or you can consider our friendship over," he pronounced angrily.

Rico looked more concerned than apologetic. "I'm sorry. More sorry, Charles, than you can ever imagine. But I can't let you be taken for a fool. And I can't let you go ahead and blindly have a baby with that woman. I have proof of what I'm saying. Hard and fast proof."

Charles's head jerked back in shock before more anger rushed in. "*Proof?* What kind of proof?" he challenged heatedly.

"Irrefutable proof."

"Such as?"

"The kind supplied by a very reputable private investigator. Facts and figures. Taped conversations with her ex-flatmates in Melbourne, people she's worked with, men she's slept with. You're welcome to hear them for yourself whenever you like. And to see the written report. Your wife *is* a fortune hunter, Charles. Make no bones about that. She openly admitted to her flatmates during her years in Melbourne that her aim in life was to marry money. You became her target after things with her previous marital candidate fell through and she made the move to Sydney.''

Charles tried to swallow the huge lump which had filled his throat but it was stuck there.

"He was her last boss," Rico swept on mercilessly. "Jonathon Hall, a reasonably successful celebrity sports manager. Though not as rich as his lifestyle indicates, which is why he ended up marrying money himself. Apparently, Dominique was livid when he dumped her. She told one of her girlfriends that the next time she wouldn't go for a guy with Hall's looks and charm. She'd try for someone older who didn't think he was God's gift to women, someone who'd be oh, so grateful to have a girl like her even look at him twice.''

Charles wanted to cry out, to scream that none of this was true. Dominique loved him.

But Rico was ruthless in his exposé of his beautiful bride's true nature. "Dominique isn't even her real name. It's something plain like Joan or Jane. I can't remember which. She changed it to Dominique when she first came to Melbourne from Tasmania when she was nineteen. Which reminds me. Her parents weren't both killed in a car accident, either, like she told you. Her mother died of cancer when Dominique was eighteen, but her father is still very much alive. Lives in a small town on the West Coast, works as a manager in one of the local mines. She's a liar and a fake, Charles, in every way."

The blood began to drain from Charles's face. He vaguely saw horror in Rico's eyes and realised he must look as shattered as he felt.

"Gee, Charles. Don't go collapsing on me. Hey, man, I didn't realise how much you loved her till this moment. I thought it was just infatuation. Man, you look terrible. What you need is a stiff drink. Come on, let's go get you one."

Charles let Rico propel him into a nearby bar, prop him up on one of the stools there and order him a brandy. He downed the drink in two quick gulps and let Rico order him another.

The brandy soon did its work and blood began slowly seeping back into his brain, his inner despair momentarily overlaid by a confused curiosity. He swivelled on the stool to face Rico once more.

"When did you find out all this?" he asked shakily. "Not before the wedding, surely."

"No. I hired the PI whilst you were on your honeymoon. The full report only came in yesterday."

"But why, Rico? Why would it even occur to you to do such a thing?"

"One of the flatmates Dominique confided in is a

cousin of mine. Claudia. She'd gone to Melbourne a couple of years ago for a change of scene after her marriage broke up. Recently, she came back to live in Sydney and was staying with one of my sisters. I was at a family get-together a few days after your wedding and was showing everyone some of the casual snapshots I'd taken when Claudia recognised Dominique. She said Dominique had this fixation about becoming really rich. Apparently, she told Claudia she could never earn enough herself in a lifetime of working for a salary, so the only solution was to marry money. Everything she did had that single aim. To catch herself a rich husband.''

Charles expressed his despair with a colourful four-letter word.

"Absolutely. I agree with you. But at least now you can see why, after what Claudia told me, I thought it was my duty as your best man to find out everything I could.''

"Which you obviously couldn't wait to pass on to me,'' Charles said bitterly. "But for what purpose, I wonder. Do you think you've done me a favour, Rico, disenchanting me like this? You could have left me in blissful ignorance. That would have been kinder.''

"I was going to for a while, believe me. But not after what you said tonight about starting a family straight away. I just couldn't stay silent and let you do that, Charles.''

"I don't see why not,'' Charles muttered bleakly.

"Fortune hunters fall into two categories,'' Rico

elaborated. "Firstly, there are the Jasmines of this world who marry you for the high life, and never have any intention of spoiling their figures having babies. Their plan is to have a ball for a while at your expense, till you start asking for a kid, like I stupidly did. Then they divorce you and take you for every penny they can in alimony. The second kind—into which your Dominique obviously falls—have a baby as soon as possible to cement their position, guaranteeing them of an even bigger settlement when they also eventually file for divorce. The child is a pawn, not the precious gift it should be. Just another little money-spinner."

Charles wanted to weep at the death of all the joyful anticipation he'd been experiencing over having a baby with Dominique.

"That's why I had to speak up, Charles," Rico said with a sympathetic hand on his shoulder. "Not just for you, but for that baby. No child deserves to be brought into this world as a bargaining chip."

Charles slowly nodded his agreement, although there was a part of him which still wished Rico had stayed silent. Now he'd probably *never* have a child.

"Get rid of her, Charles. Dump her. Divorce her. She'll be lucky to get a cent after the family law court sees all the evidence I've amassed against her."

Rico was right in his advice. But Charles knew he wouldn't do that just yet. Or was the word *couldn't*?

His hand went to his pocket to pat the box which lay there and his heart suddenly stopped breaking apart, cemented back to survival mode by an emotion far stronger than his earlier despair. Love turned to hate was an amazingly powerful motivator.

No, he wouldn't be getting rid of his beautiful new wife just yet. She had to pay for what this necklace had cost him, what *she* had cost him. His male pride demanded it. His hate insisted upon it.

Charles seethed inside when he thought of what a fool she'd made of him. A silly, blind, arrogant fool. Right from the start, she'd played him like a fiddle. Fleeing last year's Christmas party had obviously been a ploy, as had appearing reluctant to date him at first, but her spurning his advances after she finally agreed to date him had been her *coup de grâce*!

He cringed when he thought of how triumphant he'd felt when she'd said yes to his proposal of marriage. But the triumph had been all hers, not his!

How she must have chuckled behind his back when he'd decided not to sleep with her till their wedding night. Her trembling as she'd come to him that night had probably been suppressed laughter. And as for the response she'd showed to his lovemaking...

Well, he'd be having the last laugh. Let's see how good her faking ability was during the next month.

Because he was going to give himself—and her— one month. One month of vengeance.

His mouth pulled back into the travesty of a smile just thinking about some of things he planned for them. She'd probably even pretend to enjoy herself, like the mercenary manipulator she was.

"You're not going to divorce her, are you?" Rico said with a degree of stunned surprise in his voice.

Charles abandoned the rest of his second brandy—being drunk was not on tonight's agenda—then turned to his friend.

"No," he said, his voice menacingly calm. "Not just yet. But don't worry. There won't be any baby." Dominique wasn't the only one who could lie, and deceive.

Rico frowned at him. "I don't know now whether to feel sorry for you, or Dominique."

"I wouldn't waste your sympathy on her, if I were you."

"You won't do anything stupid, will you, Charles?"

"*Stupid?*"

"Like strangling her when you're making love?"

Charles laughed a cold laugh. "Do you honestly think I'd go to jail because of that little tramp? Rest assured my revenge, such as it is, won't ever take that path, or be allowed to get out of hand." As he slid off the bar stool he clamped a hand over his friend's shoulder, partly to support his own leaden legs and partly in a reassuring gesture. "Don't worry about me, Rico. I'll survive. What are you doing tomorrow?"

"Tomorrow? I'm—er—going to the races."

Charles frowned. "But none of our horses are running, are they? They're all out on spells till the spring.'' Charles and Rico usually only went to the races when they had a runner.

''Yes, but Ali has a couple of horses in with a good chance. And it's something to do,'' Rico added a bit bleakly. ''Why?''

''I was going to come over and pick up that report, and those tapes. Look, could you possibly drop them in at my place on your way to the races?''

''I'm not so sure that's such a good idea till you calm down a bit.''

''I'm perfectly calm,'' Charles bit out. ''Just bring them, will you?''

Rico sighed his reluctant resignation to his friend's request. ''Very well.''

''If you happen to speak to Dominique when you drop by, try to pretend you like her. Use some of that Latino charm you're famous for.''

''If you insist.''

''I insist. Now I must go. Dominique is probably waiting up for me, like a good little mercenary. I wouldn't like to think she'd made the effort for nothing.''

Rico's frown deepened. ''Charles, I don't like the way you're acting. It's not you. You can be a bit pompous at times, but basically you're one of the good guys, which is saying something, considering you're a billionaire *and* a businessman. Look, I know you're upset, and you have every right to be. But you're not thinking straight.''

Charles laughed, his heart like stone in his chest. "I'm thinking straighter than I have in months."

"Perhaps. But your plan of action is all wrong. Revenge never achieves anything constructive. It's a very self-destructive emotion. Trust me. I know. Just get *rid* of her!"

"Oh, I intend to. Eventually. See you tomorrow."

Rico watched his friend stalk from the bar. What had he done? He should never have opened his big mouth. He should have let sleeping dogs lie. Instead, he'd unleashed the dogs of war and who knew where it would all end?

Not happily, that was for sure.

He groaned, turned back to the bar and downed the rest of Charles's brandy.

"Get me another drink, would you?" he asked the bland-faced barman. "Not brandy this time. Bourbon. Straight. No ice."

He could afford to get drunk. He always took a taxi home on a Friday night, home to his empty apartment with its empty bed.

Still, perhaps that was better than going home to a wife like Dominique.

Or was it?

Rico glanced around the bar and saw a stunning-looking blonde of around thirty sitting at the end of the bar. When he smiled at her, she smiled back in the way women had been smiling at men for centuries. She wasn't a hooker—she looked a tad too expensive—but definitely a good-time girl.

Rico knew there was no need for him to go home to an empty bed tonight. The blonde wouldn't say no. They wouldn't even have to go far. The Regency was sure to have lots of lovely vacant rooms. May was hardly peak tourist season in Sydney and Friday night saw most of the interstate businessmen already flying home.

Only one thing stopped him. The surety that taking the blonde to bed wouldn't ease his frustration at all. Only one woman could do that at the moment. And she wasn't likely to say yes to being his bed-mate.

Renée despised him almost as much as he despised her. Why he wanted her this badly Rico could not fathom. It was perverse. And it was becoming increasingly painful.

Maybe…

He cast another look at the blonde at the end of the bar. No, she was far too much like Dominique for his liking. A man in his position couldn't afford to jump into bed with just anyone. He'd been a bit stupid in the past in this regard, and wasn't about to repeat his mistakes.

Women who were *too* beautiful were invariably trouble. He'd known Dominique was trouble the moment he clapped eyes on her. Charles had been stupid to marry her. But then, men in love were often stupid.

Rico's hand tightened around his glass. He didn't want to think about love. He didn't want to think at all!

Damn and blast. There was only one solution for

this problem, even if it was only temporary, and stupid, and futile.

Taking his bourbon with him, Rico rose and sauntered down to the end of the bar, where he slipped up onto the empty stool next to the blonde.

"You alone, honey?" he said with the slow, slightly cocky smile which captivated a worldwide female audience every week on cable television.

Her blue eyes glittered boldly up at him. "Not any more," she purred.

CHAPTER FOUR

DOMINIQUE woke with a start, followed by the swift realisation that Charles was home. She could hear him moving around the penthouse.

Immediately she sat up in the bed, plumping the pillows behind her and picking up the book which had slipped from her hand when she'd fallen asleep. She'd tried to stay awake for him, watching two movies on television and then reading one of those thrillers which claimed would keep you awake till the very last of its four-hundred pages. But this one hadn't lived up to its hype and she'd nodded off before she hit page twenty.

A glance at the bedside clock showed it was ten past one.

Not too late, she supposed. A lot of men played poker all night. Or so she'd heard.

Not that all of Charles's poker buddies were men. One of them was the very beautiful Mrs Renée Selinsky, a wealthy widow and the owner of one of Sydney's top modelling agencies called simply ''Renée's''.

Dominique had first met Mrs Selinsky at the races, a week before their wedding, and had been more than a little perturbed over the thought that Charles would be spending several hours in her company every Friday night once their honeymoon was over. The woman was not only striking to look at but obviously very clever and conspicuously unattached. She hadn't brought a partner to the races, or their wedding, making Dominique very conscious of the fact that she was footloose and fancy-free.

Dominique's first foray into real jealousy had come when she'd seen Charles and Renée talking together at their reception, which had been held here, in Charles's penthouse. The two of them had been out on the terrace, chatting intimately away and looking more than friends to Dominique's suddenly green eyes.

When she'd questioned him about this later—trying oh so hard to sound interested and not jealous—he'd told her more about his relationship with the striking Renée. The news that they'd been friends for five long years and she'd been a widow all that time did not please Dominique. Neither did her husband's joking remark that Rico called her the *merry* widow.

The nickname implied that she'd led a racy lifestyle since the death of her rich but elderly husband. Despite Renée's rather aloof manner, Dominique reckoned that the merry widow probably had had as many different lovers over those five years as she had shares in racehorses. Not having a public or permanent partner was no guarantee of celibacy these days. Dominique started thinking that maybe Charles had taken her to bed at some time. It seemed not only likely but logical, given they played cards together every week. Moving on to playing games in bed afterwards in one of those very convenient hotel rooms wasn't much of a leap of the imagination.

It had been this thought which had bothered Dominique the most about Charles going to his poker game tonight. She'd be much happier if his card cronies were all male.

Not that she'd said as much to her husband. Dominique was determined not to surrender to jealousy, which was not only new to her nature, but also highly disturbing to her psyche. Jealous women and wives loved too much, and loving anyone too much was dangerous and sometimes deadly. Dominique wanted no part of such excessive emotions.

She couldn't stop herself from loving Charles. She'd tried hard enough and failed miserably. She rigidly refused to let jealousy overtake her as well.

Nevertheless, when Charles still didn't come to bed, Dominique found herself gripping the paperback novel in her hands with white-knuckled intensity and wondering why. What was keeping him? Surely he'd seen her light under the door. Surely he'd know she was waiting up for him.

When she heard water running through the pipes, revealing that he'd turned on a tap somewhere, her heart started thudding behind her ribs, her mind tormented with black thoughts. Was he washing himself clean of that woman's scent? Wiping off all traces of her lipstick from her kisses?

Like a flash, her jealousy erupted, then raced to even greater flights of fancy. Had he even gone to play poker at all? Maybe that story was just a ruse. Maybe he spent every Friday night in bed with the merry widow, enjoying the sort of sophisticated erotic games that such a woman would be well versed in.

Rico would cover for his friend, if asked. But would Prince Ali? Dominique didn't think so. Prince Ali was not a close friend of Charles's. More of a gambling acquaintance.

Still, Dominique was hardly going to call up and cross-question such a man over his activities on a Friday night. She'd only met the prince once—the same day at the races that she'd first met Renée—and had found the Arab sheikh overwhelmingly intimidating. He had not come to their wedding, for which she was grateful. It had been difficult enough, enduring the best man's disapproval and the merry widow's disturbing presence.

The tap was turned off—wherever it was—but Charles still did not make an appearance in the master bedroom. All was suddenly silent out there. Five minutes ticked away. Then ten. Dominique was tempted to get up and go to see where Charles was and what he was doing, but something—some probably irrational fear—prevented her from leaving the bed.

I'm being ridiculous, she lectured himself. Doing what I vowed I'd never do. Screwing myself up with jealousy. Charles loves me. I know he does. He probably walked straight from the front door into the living room when he first came in, without looking down the hallway on his left, so he wouldn't have seen the bedroom light under the door. He probably thinks I'm asleep and is being considerate, using the main bathroom instead of the *en suite*. He's a very considerate man.

Dominique had one of two options. Stay where she was till he finally came to bed. Or get up and go and find him, showing him that she was wide awake and wanting him. Not for him to make love to her necessarily, if he was too tired. But his company. His conversation. His cuddles. That would do for now.

Throwing back the cream satin sheets, she slipped from the bed and hurried over to the his-and-hers walk-in wardrobes which flanked the entrance to their *en suite* bathroom. Despite never wearing anything to bed any more, she had two lovely negligée sets which she'd personally purchased with her honeymoon in mind. The nightgown she'd worn on her wedding night was long and made of pearly white satin. The one she reached for now was also long, but was made of semi-transparent black lace.

Dominique slipped it on over her nakedness, then drew on the matching robe, telling herself that she wasn't trying to seduce Charles. But the sight of herself in the full-length mirror on the back of the door mocked this thought. Seduction was the sole purpose of this kind of nightwear. It was why she'd bought it in the first place.

"Be honest," she muttered to herself. "You want Charles to make love to you. No, you *need* him to make love to you. Now. Tonight."

Sleep would be impossible if she didn't have the reassurance of his ongoing desire. A kiss and a cuddle would not be enough. She had to *know* that he hadn't been with that woman. She had to be sure.

Time was of the essence in that case. She had to hurry. Slipping her feet into the high-heeled black satin mules which complemented the elegantly sexy negligée, she hurried back to her dressing table, where she applied some lipstick and perfume, then went in search of her husband.

Charles was slumped back on the large black leather sofa which dominated the huge living room, nursing the dregs of a very large brandy and staring blankly through the picture window out at the tops of the city skyline when he realised he was no longer alone.

His head turned just far enough to view Dominique fully as she stood for a few moments in the archway that led from the main living area to the foyer.

So the gold-digger was awake again, was she? came the bitter thought even as his insides crunched down hard at the way she looked in that incredibly sexy black lace outfit.

Charles had actually gone straight to their bedroom as soon as he arrived home, eager to start exacting his revenge. But the sight of her curled up asleep had shaken his resolve. She'd looked so sweet lying there under the cream satin sheets. So soft. So...innocent.

He couldn't help it. He'd almost broken down at that juncture, staggering back out of the room to go and wash away the threatening tears. After that, he'd gone and poured himself a mind-numbing tumbler of brandy, searching for solace in its anaesthetic effect.

But there was no solace to be had when you lived with treachery; when your love was false. There was nothing but this terrible emptiness inside.

His gaze swept over her as she started floating towards him, the black lace robe flapping back to reveal a matching nightgown which was not for the faint-hearted. It was semi-transparent, the neckline cut to her navel with just a tiny satin tie keeping the lace anchored across her magnificent breasts.

A few minutes before she'd looked like an innocent young girl, lying naked and asleep in his bed. Now, with this outfit on, she looked every inch the seductress she really was.

Despite knowing her true character, Charles still felt his flesh leap to attention. Amazing, he thought. Deplorable. But exactly what he expected.

"You don't have to tell me," she purred as she came to a halt in front of him, then sank down onto the plush cream carpet at his feet. "You lost."

He stared down at her, struggling to keep the hate—and the desire—out of his face. He certainly had lost. Everything. Everything except what he could still see and touch before him. Her lips. Her breasts.

Her body, which would be ready for him. It always was.

Even as his own rapidly swelling flesh tortured him, he wondered how she managed that. What trick did she use?

"Poor darling," she crooned, leaning her cheek against his thigh and glancing up at him at the same time.

"No matter," he muttered. "It's only money." He reached down with his free hand and ran his fingers through her hair, shocked that he could still find pleasure in touching her. Why wasn't his skin crawling with revulsion?

"I haven't seen that outfit before," he remarked as he continued to sip the brandy and play with her hair. "How long have you had it?" The thought that she might have worn it to seduce the man before him made him want to rip it asunder.

She smiled up at him. Such a lovely smile. Such lovely lips.

"I bought it to wear on our honeymoon," she said, "but after our wedding night you told me you didn't want me to wear anything to bed in future. *Ever*," she added with a saucy little smile.

"So I did."

Charles toyed with the idea of demanding she never wear clothes at all when they were alone here. The penthouse was air-conditioned, after all. She wouldn't be uncomfortable provided she didn't go outside, although the lap pool *was* heated. He would definitely insist she never wear a costume when they went swimming together, in spite of the fact that the pool was in full view of several floors of nearby office buildings. If strangers could see her naked then it would test the level of her greed.

Would she comply? he speculated.

His face darkened with the surety that of course she would.

"Don't you like it?" she asked, a frown gathering on her high forehead.

Charles cleared away his own frown, replacing it with a rueful smile. "It's very sexy," he complimented. "Stand up again and let me get a better look at it."

Her instant obedience thrilled him in a highly corruptive fashion. He could get used to this, having a wife who was his own private love slave. Knowledge was power all right. He'd never have dared demand the kind of things he was going to demand, if he hadn't known what she really was.

Rico's warning that revenge was self-destructive momentarily came back to haunt him. Do you really want to take this course of action? Charles asked himself one last time. Use her beautiful body to satisfy every dark desire you can think of in your quest for vengeance?

As he stared up at her, standing there and looking down at him with pretend love in her eyes, his answer was undeniably…*yes*!

Till now he'd been such a sap, making love to her

so tenderly, so lovingly. He'd been more concerned with her pleasure than his own. He'd thought himself her perfect sexual partner during all the days and nights they'd shared. What a fool he'd been. All faked, all of it. She'd been playing a game with him; a rotten, wicked, manipulative, mercenary game.

Well, the game was his now, not hers. *She* had become the prey, not him. What a satisfying thought.

Revenge isn't destructive, Rico. It's delicious and very, very exciting.

"Take off the robe," he ordered. "Just let it fall to the floor."

She did.

Dear God...no wonder he was captivated by her. She had the most incredible body.

"Now undo the tie," he said coolly, although inside he was hot. White hot.

She complied after a moment's hesitation, her fingers shaking slightly, he noted. Clever witch. She had that move down pat. He recalled her using it on their wedding night.

"Now pull the ends back. No, further. I want to see you."

Her eyes flared wide, her fingers trembling once again as she tentatively obliged.

Her ongoing *ingénue* act began to annoy him.

"Come here," he said brusquely. "Kneel between my legs."'

Again, that brilliant hesitation. But she obeyed, as

he knew she would. She was even breathing quickly. Nice touch that.

After reaching to put his glass down on a side-table, he leant forward and took her bared nipples between his thumbs and forefingers, then squeezed and tugged them at the same time.

The sound which escaped her lips was half-gasp, half-moan.

"Did you like that?" How cool he sounded. Almost detached.

"Yes," she whispered hoarsely.

Liar!

He did it again. And again. And again.

When she started whimpering he stopped, lifting his hands to take the thin straps of the nightgown and slide them off her shoulders. Then, with one sweeping downwards motion, he stripped her of the garment, leaving her kneeling there nude before him.

Her nipples looked red against the paleness of her skin, almost as red as her lips, which were a deep scarlet. Yet they hadn't been that colour when she'd been asleep in bed, he remembered. She'd been free of make-up. Free of every artifice.

She'd certainly remedied that once she'd woken up and reverted to type.

He had to admire her tactics, however. And her acting. Anyone who didn't know the truth would think she was hopelessly turned on at this moment. Her eyes carried a slightly glazed expression and her lips had fallen temptingly apart as her breathing quickened ever further in pretend arousal.

Charles reached forward with his right hand to touch her hips, to trace their lush oval shape.

He held her eyes with his as he inserted a single finger into her mouth. Then two.

"Suck them," he whispered thickly, and began to move the two fingers in and out of her mouth.

She blinked and swayed slightly on her knees before closing her eyes and doing what he asked.

Charles's gut crunched down hard at the feel of her sucking on his fingers. It was more than a turn-on, which was the last thing he needed if he was going to remain in command of this situation.

It was then that he remembered the necklace and the scenario he'd envisaged earlier that evening.

"Charles," she moaned when he withdrew his hand to reach for his jacket, which was lying across the back of the sofa.

He almost smiled at the genuine-sounding frustration in her voice. What an actress!

"I just remembered," he said. "I bought something for you tonight." And he pulled out the long black jewelry box, flipping open the lid to show her the contents.

She gasped on cue. "Oh, Charles! You...you shouldn't have!"

She couldn't have said truer words. But he would get his money's worth in the next month, he vowed.

"But...but when did you find the time?" she asked

as she stared, first at the opals and then up at him. "I mean...I thought you were playing poker all night."

Charles was taken aback by the suspicion in her voice. Was she thinking this might be a guilt gift, that he'd been up to some kind of shenanigans instead of playing cards?

With whom, for pity's sake? He frowned as he recalled her questioning him about Renée quite closely the day of their wedding and wondered if she thought he was having an affair with the merry widow. Charles supposed duplicitous people always thought the worst of others. Dominique had no concept of what genuine love and loyalty were like. People like her lived for nothing but the acquiring of money, and material things like this necklace. If she was worried about Renée, it would only be because she didn't want to fall off the gravy train and lose her husband to another woman.

Still, Charles slotted away this weakness in Dominique, to be perhaps used at a later date.

Meanwhile, he would continue to play the besotted husband. In a fashion...

"There's a branch of Whitmore Opals in the foyer of the Regency," he reassured her as he drew the glittering and gleaming necklace from its velvet bed. "It's open till nine on a Friday night. I saw this in the window as I walked past and couldn't resist buying it for my lovely wife. Lift up your hair, darling. I want to see what it looks like on you."

This time she complied without any hesitation.

Very co-operative, Charles thought caustically.

He slid the necklace around her throat, the irony of it being a choker not lost on him. Rico had been afraid that that was what his friend would do. Choke her.

But Charles had no use for Dominique dead. He wanted her very much alive for the next month. *And* when he finally told her how long he'd known *exactly* what she was. He wanted to see the look on her face when he revealed how he'd used that knowledge, knowing that she would surrender to whatever he wanted. Like now, for instance. And shortly.

A savage satisfaction buzzed through his brain as he clipped the necklace together, then sat back to stare at her wearing his gift, and nothing else.

The sight was exquisitely decadent. And oh so erotic.

His flesh swelled even further.

"You can drop your hair back now," he said as he slowly but deliberately unzipped his trousers.

She took a moment to obey. Was she about to resist? Or to protest? She did neither, despite the fact that he had never treated her like this before. Amazing what a forty-thousand-dollar necklace could achieve.

He watched her take him into her mouth with seeming eagerness, hating her yet craving her at the same time. She was a wicked witch all right, but he was under her spell. He might always be under her sexual spell.

That was the truth of it, the awful truth. He tried to recapture his earlier vengeful anger, but it quickly became lost in his escalating need for release. With a tortured groan, he sagged back on the sofa, surrendering himself to this woman he'd foolishly married.

The feelings she engendered in him were incredibly strong, yet appallingly weak at the same time. Physically there was ecstasy, whilst mentally he was in agony. But soon Charles's emotional pain became blotted out by pleasure, the hard edge of his hate melted by the heat of her mouth and the gentle touch of her hands.

How could she *not* love him when she could make love to him like this?

He groaned and reached out to slide a caressing hand down her right arm. Her head lifted and he stared at her, at her luminescent eyes and her soft, wet lips.

"Do you want me to stop?" she said, her voice low and shaky.

Did he? Could he bear for her to continue? Could he bear for her not to?

It was then that he saw the necklace again, glittering and gleaming at him like some exotic dog collar. Suddenly, everything came back to him in a rush. All the pain of tonight's discovery. The humiliation and the hurt.

His desperation for physical release eased with the return of another need. The need for vengeance.

"No," he said, a calming wave of bitter resolve rippling through him. "No, I don't want you to stop."

Her head bent again, as he knew it would.

Obediently. Beautifully. This time he coolly played with her hair, keeping control of himself for an impressive length of time. Inevitably, however, his control began to slip, and once it did the rush towards release was swift.

But even as Charles knew he could not hold back his climax any longer, he vowed that this would not be the end of it tonight.

There would be no sleep for the wicked just yet.

And no sleep for the vengeful. Or was it the bewitched? No matter. The end result would be the same. She was going to pay for the weakness of his flesh with the weakness of hers. He would push her faking abilities to the limit. He would think of nothing but his own pleasure. He would be demanding, the male animal at his most selfish.

It would be interesting to see if she ever dared say no to him.

He doubted it.

Then tomorrow, after he'd recovered from tonight's excesses, his vengeful game would start all over again, with the stakes raised another notch.

CHAPTER FIVE

DOMINIQUE hummed happily as she stepped under a hot shower the next morning and lifted her face to the spray. It was almost ten o'clock and Charles was still asleep in their bed, out like a light.

And no wonder.

Last night had been incredible!

Although initially startled by her husband's unexpected transformation from a gentle lover to one she'd never known before, Dominique had soon found herself more turned on than ever before. She'd been with him all the way, from the episode in the living room, to the imaginative one in this shower afterwards, and finally a torrid session back in the bedroom.

She couldn't help hoping Charles would lose at poker every Friday night if that was what it did to him! Only sheer physical exhaustion had stopped him in the end and they'd both fallen asleep with their bodies still fused together, spoon fashion, Charles's lips buried in her hair.

And her breasts…

Dominique stopped humming and glanced downwards. She flinched a little as she ever so gently touched her breasts. They were very tender indeed.

Still, they'd recover! She would rub some soothing lotion on them later.

Charles had just got a bit carried away, well, more than a bit, actually. As wildly exciting as the experience had been, Dominique wasn't sure if she could cope with that level of raw passion every night of the week!

Whatever, last night had at least put paid to any silly notion she'd been harbouring that her husband was having an affair with the merry widow on a Friday night. No man could have done what he'd done for as long as he did it after being with another woman beforehand. Not unless he'd sold his soul to the devil.

No, she had nothing to worry about in that regard. And nothing to be jealous over when he played poker on a Friday night any more.

Dominique began to hum again as she started washing.

Charles woke groggily to a hangover and the sound of a hair-dryer in the bathroom. Rolling over with a groan, he saw that it was going on eleven. Another groan escaped his parched lips. He had to get up. Rico could be here shortly.

But he just didn't have the energy to rise. Last night had totally flattened him.

Last night…

It hadn't quite worked out as he'd planned. What had begun as an act of vengeance had eventually changed to the most exciting sexual encounter of his life!

That woman was more than a witch. She was the devil incarnate.

The sudden silence in the bathroom was soon followed by the door opening. And there she was, wrapped neck to knee in a cream towelling bathrobe, her cheeks glowing, her golden hair sleekly blow-dried and falling halfway down her back.

"So you're awake at last," she threw at him with a saucy smile as she padded, barefoot, across the plush cream carpet.

Everything in the master bedroom and *en suite* bathroom was cream, with gold trim, the penthouse having come fully furnished when Charles had bought it. He'd always thought the overall décor a bit bland, especially in here. But Dominique loved it. She thought it elegant.

He watched her sit down on the cream and gold brocade-covered stool which faced the curved cream dressing-table in the corner then pick up a jar from amongst the wide selection of jars and bottles lined up underneath the three-sided mirror.

Charles had realised soon after they were married that Dominique took skin care and make-up very seriously. As she did keeping her body fit and toned. The exercise routine she put herself through every other day in the gym of whatever hotel they were staying at during their honeymoon was gruelling. Charles's choice of exercise was swimming, which he found both energising and relaxing. He wasn't interested in big muscles, just staying lean and healthy.

Charles hadn't seen anything wrong with his new bride's passion with physical perfection before last night's revelations. Now he realised she worked as hard as she did because she viewed her body as a weapon to get what she wanted in life. Looking fabulous had been a necessity in her quest for marriage to a rich man.

Charles had to concede that the first thing which had attracted him to Dominique was her face and figure. Did that make him as shallow as she was? Or just a typical male, more susceptible to visual attractiveness than the female of the human species?

"I was just thinking in the shower," she said as she began unscrewing the lid of the jar, "that if losing at cards always turns you into a primitive beast, I should hope for you to lose every Friday night. Though perhaps not," she added with a rueful laugh as she scooped some cream out with her fingertips. "I don't think my poor nipples could take it. They're terribly sore this morning. You won't be able to touch them for at least a few…hours," she finished, flashing him a wickedly sexy smile in the mirror.

Charles gritted his teeth and watched, his head thudding dreadfully and his mouth as dry as a desert, whilst she slid her hand into the front of the towelling robe and started rubbing the lotion over her right breast and nipple.

"So what are we going to do today?" she asked

as her tormenting hand went round and round. "After I've cooked you breakfast, of course. But can you manage breakfast, darling? You're looking a little peaked over there."

"I'm wrecked," he admitted curtly. "You've wrecked me."

She laughed. "*I've* wrecked *you*! Might I remind you it was *you* who started that whole episode last night? All I came out for was a kiss and a cuddle."

"In that black lace outfit?" he mocked. "Come, now, Dominique, you got exactly what you wanted. Or are you saying you didn't enjoy yourself?"

He watched her reaction to this but she just laughed again. He actually wanted to strangle her then, which reminded him of Rico.

"I have to get up," he muttered. "Rico's due here shortly."

The dismay on her face at this news didn't elude him. She *knows* Rico knows what she is, Charles realised.

"What on earth for?" she said. "And why didn't you tell me before this? You could have mentioned it last night."

His smile was on the cold side. "I hardly had time to talk to you last night. We were busy doing other things. Still, it's nothing for you to worry about." Not yet, anyway. "It isn't a social call. He's just dropping off a report."

"What kind of report?"

"A report from a private investigator."

Did she grow pale at this pronouncement? Or was he just imagining it?

"Rico hired one for me whilst we were away on our honeymoon," he elaborated. "To check up on one of my employees." Again, he watched her closely.

"Really? What's the poor fellow done to make you do something as drastic as that?"

"You've assumed it was a man."

She shrugged, her attitude seemingly nonchalant. He must have imagined her reacting guiltily before. Clearly, she had no idea he was talking about her.

"Most of your employees are men," she said. "Especially in the higher-up positions."

True. She'd been one of the few female executives he'd ever hired. It wasn't a chauvinist decision, just the way it had worked out. Most of the applicants for executive positions were men, and most were more qualified than the women. He'd made an exception in Dominique's case because when he'd read her CV he'd admired her drive and ambition. He hadn't realised at the time just how driven and ambitious she was!

God, but he wished she'd stop rubbing that stuff into her nipples! It was killing him. But be damned if he was going to touch her again this morning.

So much for his vengeful ideas of having her parade around naked for him all the time. He'd end up wanting her all the time. Him, having to listen to her fake moans, whilst his own flesh responded just the same. Blindly. Helplessly. Stupidly!

His so-called vengeance had to have a rest for a few hours at least, which meant he had to get out of here for a while. Out in public her body would be well covered and the opportunities to surrender to temptation were limited. As much as Charles had fantasised about having sex with her out in the pool with lots of office workers looking on, he knew now he would never do anything like that, because the humiliation would again be his more than hers. Dominique was his wife, for pity's sake, and whilst she was his wife he would treat her with respect under the gaze of others, or risk having no respect for himself.

"What did he do?"

For a few confusing seconds, Charles had no idea what she was talking about. And then he remembered.

He looked into her curious and seemingly innocent blue eyes and tried to imagine how she'd react when he finally told her *she'd* been the subject of the investigation. Would she deny everything, then try to persuade him of her love with her body?

Oh, yes. That was exactly what she'd do. Charles had to confess he was looking forward to that moment. He'd save up the darkest of his desires for when she was at her most desperate. That kind of encounter would be real vengeance.

"Nothing strictly illegal," he replied. "But when you discover that an employee whom you promoted to a position of absolute trust has lied to you, more than once, you start to wonder, and to worry.''

''Lied about what?''

''I don't think I can reveal that. There might be a court case at some time in the future.'' Dominique was sure to sue for alimony when he finally asked for a divorce.

''But I thought you said he did nothing illegal,'' she argued. ''Besides, I'm your wife. Surely you can tell me.''

''I will,'' he hedged. ''After I've read the report myself. At the moment, I only know generalities, not details. Suffice to say that it all sounds very damning indeed. Meanwhile, I must get myself into that shower and get dressed. You too, darling. Once Rico has gone I think we'll go somewhere for brunch then out for some serious house-hunting.''

Her face understandably lit up at this news. It was probably one of her goals, being the mistress of a multimillion-dollar harbourside mansion where she could give extravagant parties dressed in her designer gowns. After all, what was the point in marrying money if you couldn't display the fruits of your labours?

And, by God, she had worked hard to catch him and even harder since the wedding. He had to give her credit for that. It couldn't be easy having to pretend she loved him twenty-four hours a day, and now to smile at him with sore nipples...

Charles threw back the bedclothes and headed for the bathroom.

Dominique sighed as she watched Charles hurry into the *en suite*. The last person she wanted to see this morning was Enrico Mandretti. She couldn't stand the way that man looked at her when Charles wasn't looking, as if she was some sort of nasty creature who'd just crept out from under a rock.

Judging by Charles's speed, Rico must be due here shortly. She would have to hurry and get dressed herself. No way did she want to answer the door in nothing but a bathrobe. She knew exactly what kind of look *that* would get!

Rising from the dressing-table, she hurried into her walk-in wardrobe, swiftly selecting a camel-coloured trouser suit which had a thigh-length jacket which minimised rather than emphasised her curvy figure. What was fine for Charles's eyes wasn't for his sneering best man's.

Back at her dressing-table five minutes later, she swept her hair up into a loose twist and applied the lightest and most natural of make-ups. Even her lipstick echoed the natural colour of her lips. Just a touch of mascara. No eye-shadow or eye-liner. She was slipping simple gold studs into her ears when the doorbell rang.

"Oh, damn," she said, hearing the water in the shower still running. Charles must have shaved first.

She had no option but to go and answer the door herself. Steeling herself for some even more overt disapproval than usual, Dominique walked reluctantly from the bedroom and along the hallway to the penthouse's elegant foyer. The heels of her Italian leather ankle boots clacked on the foyer tiles as she crossed to the front door. But she didn't whisk it open straight away. First, she gave a final check to her appearance in one of the wall-mounted mirrors which flanked the front door, after which she peered through the built-in security peep-hole to make sure it *was* Rico.

It was.

Unfortunately.

Dominique unlocked, then opened the door, by which time she'd dredged up a polite smile.

"Hello, Rico," she said. "Come on in."

He strode in, his broad-shouldered six-foot-two frame made even more menacing—or attractive, depending on your point of view—by a suave black suit and a matching black crew-necked top. His longish and incorrigibly wavy black hair was slicked back from his slightly large but broodily handsome face and he was sporting what was these days called designer stubble on his chin.

He was one of the most famous Italian cooks on TV in the world today. Which was perverse, since he wasn't a trained chef at all, according to Charles. Or even born in Italy. The two men had discovered a mutual love of gambling and soon became firm friends.

"Charles is in the shower, I'm sorry," was her first

remark. She sounded defensive and not at all apologetic.

"At *this* hour?" he returned, glancing at his watch.

Dominique couldn't help it. She crossed her arms and glared at him. She didn't like Rico any more than he liked her and she was not going to pretend any different.

"It's Saturday," she said coolly. "Charles can stay in bed all day if he likes. What's it to you, anyway?"

Rico's teeth clamped down hard in his jaw. Charles had asked him to be polite today. But it was going to be impossible. Best he just drop off the damned report and get the hell out of here before he said something he shouldn't.

There was nothing more he could do for his friend, anyway. He'd warned him to cut his losses and get rid of this conniving little con-artist. But no, the besotted fool had to keep hanging in there for a while longer, didn't he, all the time kidding himself that he was having some kind of pathetic revenge?

Maybe, when Charles read this report for himself and heard the damning evidence on the tapes, he'd change his mind and dump the woman. Pronto!

And maybe not.

Rico looked Dominique up and down and conceded that she was one hot-looking babe, despite her obviously trying to play her figure down somewhat this morning for whatever reason. But he'd seen her in clothes other than the conservative outfit she was wearing at this moment, and she had the sort of curves designed to make men's heads turn.

At her sharp reply, his own tongue was eager for a workout. "Charles usually does twenty laps of his pool every morning before breakfast," he countered. "I've never known him to be up later than seven. But, of course, that was before he got married. Before…you."

"Meaning what?" she snapped.

"Meaning things have changed and they'll never be the same again. Tell Charles I couldn't stay. The first race is at twelve-fifteen today. Here's the report I promised him." And he handed her the bulky envelope which contained more than enough evidence to have her out on her ear without a single cent.

But would Charles use it?

Rico certainly hoped so. If he didn't, he just might have to do something about this situation himself. He couldn't let this lady continue to con his best friend. Charles had his faults but he was a genuine gentleman, highly respected by everyone who knew him. Rico had known him for several years now, and would have trusted him with his life. He wasn't about to let Charles throw away any more of his life—and his pride—on some mercenary-minded vamp.

"Oh, yes," she said smugly. "The report. Charles told me all about it."

Rico was stunned. "He *told* you about it?"

She clasped the envelope to her chest, her eyes

flashing defiance at him. "Yes, of course. Why shouldn't he? I'm his wife."

Rico couldn't make held or tail of what was going on here.

"Why look so surprised?" she threw at him. "Have you forgotten I used to work for Charles myself? Don't you think I'd care if one of the people he'd employed and trusted turned out to be a con-artist and a liar?"

Aah…now Rico understood. Charles had invented a half-truth story to explain the report. How clever of him. How devious. How…devilish.

Maybe he was worrying about his friend for nothing. Maybe Charles was more than capable of handling his money-grabbing wife and having some rightful vengeance at the same time. Rico understood all about rightful vengeance. He was Italian, after all.

"You know, Rico," she said, those big blue eyes of hers glittering away frostily, "I'm fed up to the teeth with your looking down your supercilious Italian nose at me. What *is* your problem with me? Is it that you think I'm some sort of fortune hunter who's only with Charles for his money? Charles told me about your experience with your ex-wife, so I suppose that has to be it. But let me tell you this: I *love* my husband. No, that's understating things. I *adore* him. He's my life. What worries him worries me. What distresses him distresses me. So do me a favour in future and keep your cynical suspicions to yourself!"

Rico stared at her. What a tiger she was when crossed! And how convincing she sounded. If he didn't know better, he might have believed her.

He'd have to warn Charles never to let things go to court, because some damned fool male judge just *might* believe her. She could argue that she'd been a fortune hunter up till the moment she met Charles, then whammo, true love struck and she changed overnight into a loyal and ever-devoted wife.

Men could be suckers when it came to a beautiful woman. He knew that only too well.

"Don't forget to give Charles that report," Rico said with a rueful little smile. "Tell him I'll give him a call tonight and we'll discuss it. See you, Dominique."

Dominique pulled a face at his broad back as he walked away.

Wretched man. And a troublemaking one too. If he had his way, he'd break my marriage up. All he wants is his best mate back, so that he can go places with him. He doesn't give a damn about Charles's happiness, only his own.

"Was that Rico?"

Dominique spun to see Charles hurrying along the hallway towards her, pulling on a jumper as he did so. She quickly closed the door to prevent his running after the man. It would only take a few seconds and Rico would be on his way downstairs. Their private lift would be there, at the ready, for him.

"Yes, he had to dash," she replied. "He said he

was late for the races. Here's the report he left.'' And she handed the bulky envelope to her disgruntled-looking husband.

''No other messages?''

''He said he'd ring you tonight.''

Charles nodded, then stared down at the envelope which he was turning over and over in his hands.

''You're not going to read that right now, are you?'' she asked. ''You must be hungry. I know I am.''

He glanced up, and smiled at her. ''You know, you have an amazing appetite for a girl who worries about her figure like you do.''

Dominique shrugged. ''I work hard so that I can enjoy the good things in life.''

''Yes. Yes, I can see that. In that case, I'll just put this in my den and we can be on our way.''

''On our way where?'' she asked as she trailed after him down the other hallway which led to the room Charles liked to call his den. But it was more of a study-cum-office, fresh and modern with pale grey walls, carpet and furniture. The interior designer who'd done out this penthouse obviously had a thing for each room having the same colour throughout. Even the ceiling in here was painted the same pale grey. The vertical blinds too. Charles wasn't all that keen on the décor but Dominique liked clean, simple lines and pale colours. She rarely wore bright colours herself, preferring neutrals and pastels.

''I thought we might stroll down to the Rocks area

and have brunch there,'' Charles said, tossing the envelope onto the top of his grey desk before turning to
draw her into his arms. "Then I'll call up a real-estate
agent I know and have him show us some houses.
How's that?"

"Wonderful!" She cupped his cheeks and kissed
him.

Charles's heart lurched, reminding him of his ongoing vulnerability to this woman. He shouldn't have
taken her in his arms. It had just seemed a natural
thing to do. He almost kissed her back, wanting to
feel the soft surrender of her mouth under his, wanting to forget everything but the pleasure to be found
in her body.

But he didn't. Still, it was a close call, Charles
having a struggle to resist temptation. Hopefully, after
he read that report tonight his desire for revenge
would be right back on track.

"Let's go," he said brusquely and, drawing back,
he took her elbow and propelled her out of the room.

CHAPTER SIX

"So what do you think?" Charles asked, then waited for Dominique to gush.

It was four in the afternoon and this was the third harbourside property the agent had taken them to inspect, but the first to be empty of all furniture and inhabitants. It was brand-new, and had taken two years to build, the builder having bought an old dump on the site which he'd then torn down to build a home more in keeping with this exclusive area. The asking price reflected the bank balances of the neighbours. Fifteen million dollars.

"Well?" Charles prompted when Dominique remained silent.

They were standing in the huge living area at one of the bay windows which overlooked the terrace and the resort-size pool. Further on were the formal gardens and on one side the maintenance-free tennis court.

There was no yacht moored at the private jetty which jutted out into Sydney Harbour at the bottom of the gently sloping lawns, but Charles had no doubt Dominique would want one of those too, in due course.

Her lovely high forehead crinkled into a frown. "I

don't know, Charles. It's so big! I mean...I'm sorry, but I don't think I want a house as big as this.''

Charles couldn't believe it. The place was gold-digger paradise. It had everything. And all within a stone's throw of the city.

''I want a real family home,'' she went on, ''not a showplace.''

Charles stared at her. *This*, from a woman who'd only married him for his money? Something wasn't right here. What game was she playing now?

''But we could throw some wonderful parties here,'' he pointed out, waving his arm around the luxurious and spacious living area.

Dominique looked surprised. ''I didn't think parties would be such a big priority with you from now on. I thought you wanted a family life.''

''I did. I *do*,'' he insisted. ''But that doesn't mean I won't have to entertain sometimes. If you're worried about the price then don't be. I can easily afford it.''

''What? Oh, yes, yes, I'm sure you can, but that's not the point. Can I be blunt, Charles?''

''By all means.''

''I'm sorry, but I just don't like this place. It's over-the-top and not you at all.''

''Not me...''

''Yes, you're not a show-off. You're rich, yes, but you don't flaunt it. Your penthouse is fabulous but it's not decked out like some rich playboy's pad. I'll bet you bought it more for its convenient location than any other reason.''

Actually, she couldn't have been more right. Charles had always hated to waste time on travelling to and from the office. Before the penthouse he'd lived on the other side of the harbour on one of the far northern beaches, and had resented the time it took him every morning and evening, battling the traffic which flooded across the bridge.

"I can understand you want a quality home," Dominique continued. "But this isn't a home. It's just a setting for the kind of man who would want to live here. Maybe you should tell Rico it's on the market. He'd be the perfect owner."

"You really don't like Rico, do you?"

"What came first, the chicken or the egg?" she countered. "He disliked me at first sight. It's difficult to like someone who shows you nothing but disrespect."

Charles was alarmed. "Rico's been openly disrespectful to you?" He knew he should have been there when Rico arrived this morning. But he'd been in the darned shower.

"No, I guess not," she admitted, somewhat reluctantly. "He's clever enough not to be openly rude. But I can feel his disapproval just the same. He thinks I'm after your money."

Charles sighed his relief. Rico hadn't really said anything, then. "Rico is going through a very cynical phase where women are concerned."

"Don't make excuses for him," she snapped.

"I'm not making excuses. I'm just explaining

where he's coming from. He was very hurt by his ex. She spent his money like water whilst he was married to her, flatly refused to have children, then ripped him off for more money during the divorce.''

''Maybe she didn't want children. She does have that right, you know.''

''Yes, but she'd said she did want children *before* the wedding. Remember that Rico's Italian. He'd never knowingly marry a woman who didn't want children.''

''I see. Well, I guess he was hurt. But that's no reason to take it out on me. Besides, I *want* to have your children. Have you told him that?''

''Actually, I have.'' And she wouldn't be too thrilled with his reaction, Charles thought wryly. But he could see now that Rico had to be right in his assessment of the type of gold-digger Dominique was. Her game plan was nothing like Jasmine's. Her plan was to play the devoted wife and even have a baby, after which she would be in an invincible position when it came to demanding a huge divorce settlement. After all, she would be the mother of his child.

The thought popped into his head that she might be vetoing this property because she didn't want him tying up so much cash in a house which might prove difficult to sell. Buyers of fifteen-million-dollar harbourside mansions didn't come along every day of the week. This particular property had been on the market for a few months already.

Charles had difficulty hiding the bitterness his

thoughts evoked. It welled up inside him, like bile on the rise. How could someone so beautiful be so wicked?

And she looked extra-beautiful today, dressed as she was in that simple yet classy outfit. He found her no less sexy for her having hidden her voluptuous curves. Perversely, it made him want her all the more.

Whenever he looked at her, he kept thinking how much he would enjoy stripping her of that super-conservative suit later this evening; how he would insist she swim with him in the nude, under the moonlight. The nearby offices would be shut, so there were no worries about their being seen. He could do exactly as he liked.

His heart thudded at the thought, and the thought of all the other scenarios to come.

The time had arrived, he realised, to make sure that no baby would be conceived during his month of vengeance. The real-estate agent was outside, taking a call on his cellphone. They had time to talk.

"Speaking of having children, darling, would you mind if we put off trying for a baby for a little while?"

His request clearly dismayed her.

"But why?" she protested. "I thought you were as anxious as me to get started on a family."

"I'm only talking about a month or two." He smiled and took her in his arms. A painful necessity if he was to act normally around her. "Call me selfish but I want you to myself for a little while longer. I don't want you feeling sick every morning and telling me to get lost. We've only been married a month, after all, and it's not as though we were sleeping together before the wedding. I can't get enough of you at the moment, my darling,'' he said truthfully. ''Why do you think I'm taking next week off work? It isn't only to look at houses. Be patient and try to understand. I'm a red-blooded man in love for the first time in his life. I'm sure my needs will lessen in time...''

Hell, he hoped so or he might go insane. Just taking her into his arms had made his desire move from his brain to his body. The ache was unbearable.

She slanted a coy look up at him. ''Do you want me to keep taking the Pill the way I have been?''

''Can you?'' During their honeymoon, she'd skipped the week of white pills which brought on a period, going straight on to the next month's red pills. Her doctor suggested the idea, knowing she was going away on her honeymoon.

''It shouldn't be any problem for another cycle. But after that, I'm stopping. You're not getting any younger, Charles, and neither am I. I *want* your baby. Fair enough?''

Something twisted inside Charles. Oh, if only she was speaking the truth. But Rico was probably right. What she wanted was an insurance policy.

''If you insist,'' he said.

''I insist. Now, let's go find the real-estate agent and see if he has something more cosy on his books.''

"Cosy," Charles repeated drily. "She wants cosy."

Dominique smiled. "Cosy compared to this, anyway. I won't object to water views, or a pool in the back yard. But I don't want it to be so large that we'd have to employ live-in staff to look after it. I would hate that. I wouldn't mind a cleaner coming in one day a week, like you have at the penthouse. But on the whole I want to look after my own home. And you, my love. I didn't get married to have someone else do all the cooking and cleaning. Which reminds me, I don't want to go out to dinner tonight. I want to cook us a meal at home. Your cupboards and freezer are full of ingredients and I'm a really good cook, even if I say so myself."

Charles didn't give a hoot about dinner at that moment. His hunger went in an entirely different direction.

Still, having her cook for him was far better than having to sit through a slow meal at a restaurant.

"I didn't get married just to be your legal mistress, you know," she tossed off airily.

Too bad, he thought. Because that was exactly what she was going to be for the next month. He'd paid for the privilege of unlimited access to her body and that was exactly what he was going to have! Still, if she wanted to throw in some home cooking then he wasn't about to object.

Charles glanced at his watch. "Time's getting on. It'll be dark soon. The days are so short at this time of year. How about we put off any more house-hunting till tomorrow and I take you home? We could relax and have a few drinks together whilst you wave your magic wand in the kitchen.''

She laughed. ''You don't fool me, Charles Brandon. It's not wine or food you want.''

He smiled. ''You've caught me out.''

''That's all right, darling,'' she whispered, then reached up on tiptoe to press a softly teasing kiss on his lips. ''I feel exactly the same way.''

His arms swept around her, pulling her hard against him, flattening her breasts against his chest and wrapping the soft swell of her stomach around his by now bursting erection. Their eyes locked and for the life of him, he could have sworn he was looking at real passion in hers. The way they dilated, then smouldered.

''Charles,'' she choked out, sounding almost desperate with desire.

It came to him then that maybe, just maybe, he'd touched something in her that no man had ever touched before. Maybe she wasn't faking. Maybe she'd become a victim of her own cold-blooded plan.

He didn't imagine for one second that she loved him. Women like her didn't love anything except money. But he supposed even the most mercenary creature was capable of enjoying sex. Rico had never said Jasmine faked it in bed. Rico had always believed his ex liked having sex with him.

Another thought followed, a much darker but more

logical thought. Maybe their passionate lovemaking last night had unexpectedly turned her on?

Charles decided to test his theory, right then and there.

"You do realise I can't wait till I get you home," he told her, and watched her lips fall apart. Shock, he wondered? Or instant arousal?

"I'll tell the agent we're going upstairs to look at the main bathroom once more," he went on, his own heart racing. "You won't have to get fully undressed. He'll never know. And if he does, who cares?"

"But…"

"No buts," he said forcefully. "Let's go."

CHAPTER SEVEN

"YOU'RE angry with me," were her first words when they finally got home.

Charles closed the door behind them then looked deep into her agitated eyes. "No," he said quite truthfully. "I'm not angry with you." Bewildered was more the word.

She'd refused to let him make love to her when he'd taken her up to the *en suite* bathroom in that house. Quite adamantly. She'd stated she couldn't possibly with that man downstairs. When he'd pressed the issue, she'd seemed so genuinely distressed that he'd stopped. Maybe she'd been acting. Maybe not. He could no longer tell.

Whatever, so much for his theory. Or his expectation that she'd do anything he asked. Clearly, there was a limit to her co-operation.

"You had every right to refuse," he said, doing his best to sound calm rather than confused. "I would never force you to do anything you didn't like."

She shook her head. "You don't understand. It wasn't that I didn't want to. I did. Too much," she muttered under her breath as she turned away from him and began to walk disconsolately across the foyer.

He grabbed her by the shoulders and spun her back round to face him. "What? What did you say?"

Her eyes whipped up to his. "You heard me, Charles," she cried. "I wanted you to do it, *way* too much. I've been wanting you way too much ever since I met you. I…I've never felt anything like what I feel when I'm with you. It frightens me sometimes. I'm not used to not having control over my life, or my feelings. Do you understand what I'm saying, Charles?"

"Yes," he choked out as a wild elation rushed through his veins.

She *did* feel something for him. Maybe not love, but lust, yes. And right from the start. She hadn't lied about that. She'd wanted him as she'd never wanted any other man. He could feel her trembling even now, feel her fear of losing control.

She *was* putty in his hands, as he'd once imagined.

What a wildly corrupting thought! Much better than thinking he could make her do what he wanted through greed. Greed had obviously taken a backstep in her life whilst desire reigned supreme.

His hands tightened on her shoulders as he dragged her mouth up to his, his kiss savage and uncompromising. She stiffened but she didn't struggle and soon she was responding to the fierce probing of his tongue. Not till he was confident that her control was totally shattered did Charles lift his mouth from hers. His own control began to slip at the way she just stood there, eyes dazed, whilst he stripped her naked.

"Charles," she whimpered when he finally drew her quivering nudity against his still fully clothed body.

"Soon," he promised thickly. "Soon."

There was something incredibly erotic about just holding her like that. Even more so when he noticed their reflection in the wall mirrors which flanked the front door. Her buttocks were so pale against his dark grey trousers. He ran his large brown hands over the soft globes of flesh, lifting them, squeezing them. She buried her face into his neck and moaned. The ache in his own flesh was acute but he was determined not to rush things. He wanted to wallow in his new discovery that she wasn't pretending, at least where sex was concerned. Finally, he turned her round so that he could see himself caress her.

"Oh," she gasped once her glazed eyes connected to their mirrored images, groaning hard, then flinching slightly when he rubbed the centre of his palms over her already hard nipples.

"Oh, Dominique!" he cried, his hands dropping away. She was obviously still very sore after last night. He shuddered at the thought.

She blinked, then picked his hands up and put them right back on her breasts. "They're all right," she said thickly. "They don't hurt that much. Don't stop, Charles. Please don't stop."

Her blind excitement excited him unbearably, but he couldn't bring himself to touch her breasts again. Now he remembered how sore she'd said her nipples had been this morning. At the same time, he did what she wanted. He did not stop, his hands travelling down over her tensely held stomach, pressing her bottom back against his rigid sex, sliding his fingers down towards the V of blonde curls between her legs.

"Oh, God, yes," she begged, even before his fingertips slipped through her dampness in search of that spot which invariably sent her over the edge. He was perilously close to his own edge by then. If he moved his hips, he'd be a goner. He kept himself deathly still whilst his hand moved on.

Her whole body froze, her head falling back against his shoulder, her mouth gaping wide. She trembled violently, her cry the cry of a lost soul, her lower body jerking against him.

Charles couldn't help it. Hearing and feeling her was bad enough. Watching it in the mirror at the same time was too much. His release was involuntary, and for a few moments all thought ceased. But as soon as the wild heat of the moment subsided, his mind began to torture him.

What *was* he going to do with this woman, this woman he still craved? There was no point in kidding himself. His love for her hadn't turned to hate and his need for cold, hard vengeance was already beginning to wane. His initial desire to make her pay had just been a reaction to finding out she was a gold-digger. He'd wanted to strike back as any man would.

But everything had changed now, he realised as he swept her limp body up into his arms. She did have feelings for him. Maybe they were largely sexual but so what? A man could go a long way to find a wife who responded the way she did. So she wanted his money as well as his body. He could learn to live with that. And she was at least willing to give him a child.

Of course, Rico would say he was a fool to even consider not divorcing her. A desperate, Dominique-obsessed fool. And maybe Rico was right. But Rico *was* going through an extra-cynical phase. Dominique might not have any intention of asking for a divorce after she had his baby. She might be quite content to hitch a ride on his gravy train for life. If so, why would he want to get rid of her? Hell, he *loved* her.

Yes, but she doesn't love *you*, came back the argument for the defence. Her fancying you was just a twisted act of fate. She still lied to you, deceived you, played you for a fool. Can you really live with that forever without saying anything to her, without letting her know you know the truth?

Charles wasn't sure. His pride had always been both an asset and a weakness where he was concerned. He would hate to think she really thought him a fool.

Clearly, it was high time for him to read that report for himself, see in detail the evidence against her. Then he could make a more informed decision.

Meanwhile, he had to do something about the state of his underwear. ''I have to shower and change,'' he said as he carried her down the hallway which led to the master bedroom. "And you, madam, have to put some clothes on."

"Why?" she murmured dreamily, and he laughed.

"Because having you naked is an irresistible temptation. And I have to go read that report. Didn't you say Rico was going to ring me later this evening? He'll want to know what I think of it and I can hardly tell him I haven't had time."

"You pander to Rico too much," she said.

"He's my best friend. And a very astute businessman. I like to discuss things with him."

Her eyes suddenly cleared of their passionate haze to show the intelligence which lay behind her beauty. "I'm your wife and not exactly a dummy. Why not discuss that report with me? After all, I worked for Brandon Beer as well."

"Yes, but not any more," he said, and gave her a light peck on the forehead. "I don't want you worrying your pretty little head about business matters."

Her nose crinkled up. "Don't start treating me like some blonde bimbo, Charles. I wouldn't like that."

"What a shame. I always wanted a blonde bimbo for a wife." He smiled in an effort to make light of their discussion, and to deflect her away from talking about that report. He sincerely wished he'd never told her about the darned thing now.

"You don't mean that," she chided.

"Don't be too sure," came his laughing reply, and, dumping her in the middle of the bed, he whirled and strode straight for the bathroom.

"What would you like to have for dinner?" she called after him before he could escape.

You again, came the automatic thought.

"Anything," he called over his shoulder. "I'm easy."

Too easy where you're concerned, he realised bitterly. Any other man would have tossed her out on her ear by now. But what was he doing? Making excuses for her, clinging to any train of thought which would accommodate his desperate desire to keep her as his wife, and to keep having her body. It had to stop. He had to read that report, talk to Rico again for some balance of opinion, then hopefully make some tough decisions.

As soon as the bathroom door was safely shut, Dominique rolled over on the cream satin quilt and buried her face in her hands. She was perilously close to crying, yet she wasn't sure why. There was no real reason for her to be afraid like this again, no reason to worry that her marriage was heading for disaster.

Yet she *was* worried.

Was it because of the kind of sex Charles was suddenly wanting? Or was the fear still her own inner panic over loving anyone as much as she loved her husband?

She'd been cripplingly close to letting him have his way with her this afternoon in that ghastly mausoleum of a house. His forcefulness had excited her, there was no doubt about it. On top of that, they hadn't made love all day and she'd been wanting him badly. Clearly, she'd become addicted to his touch.

What had just happened out in the foyer was a perfect example of his power over her body, and her ever-escalating vulnerability to his. That was why she'd said no up front this afternoon. Because she'd been afraid that once Charles started, she would have been incapable of refusing him and she soon would not have cared if the real-estate agent *had* walked in on them.

That kind of loving was anathema to her. She wanted to flee from it, yet at the same time she was perversely drawn to it. She couldn't help being attracted to the woman she became in his arms, the uncontrollably passionate creature who was nothing like the cold-blooded mercenary-driven robot she'd become over the years. It was a relief to be driven by desire alone, and not the desire for money.

Money...

Dominique rolled over and stared up at the ceiling.

Did she even want money any more? Yes, yes, of course she must. Nothing would ever rid her of the fear of being poor. Her worrying that she would have married Charles, poor or not, was a really stupid train of thought. Charles was Charles because he *was* successful and smart. A man amongst men in every sense of the word, impressive and decisive, with a strong sense of self which she found overwhelmingly sexy.

Charles...

She needed him, needed his arms around her and

his mouth on hers. Only then would she feel safe again—and completely satisfied.

Tears flooded her eyes as the need to be with the man she loved struggled with her shame at appearing so needy in his eyes. It was no wonder he'd been surprised when she'd rejected him this afternoon. When had she ever said no to whatever he wanted? And he was wanting more and more from her lately. Last night seemed to have released a different Charles, a darker, more demanding man. What would she say when he made further demands?

Dominique was afraid her answer would always be yes.

With a raw cry of defeat she sprang off the bed and hurried to the bathroom door. Her grimace as the knob turned easily in her hand reflected her inner torment. Why hadn't he locked it? Why did he have to make it so easy for her to give in to this escalating weakness?

She opened the door and walked in, each step an exercise in humiliation. The tears spilled over and ran down her cheeks.

She found Charles standing under a stinging shower spray, his head bowed, his palms flat against the cream tiles. He didn't see her standing there, watching him through the steamed-up screen. Her sliding back the shower door sent his head jerking round.

"What the...?" He stared at her tear-stained face, his eyes flaring wide. "What is it? What's wrong?"

What's wrong? Dear God, if only he knew...

"I...I need you to make love to me, Charles," she choked out. "Now. Properly. Please..."

A tremor rippled down Dominique's spine when she saw his body respond to her plea, instinctively, automatically, as if he had no say in the matter. Her eyes widened at the realisation that he was as much in her power as she was in his.

"You want me too," she whispered, awed by his instant erection.

"Always," he said thickly, and held out his hand to her.

She placed her hand in his, then smiled shakily at him through her tears. "You do love me, don't you?"

"How can you doubt it?" he said, and pulled her into the heated enclosure.

I won't in future, she vowed as he kissed her, the hunger in his mouth as reassuring as the strong arms around her. I'm going to stop this negative nonsense once and for all. I'm going to be happy and secure in Charles's love from now on. No more fear. No more worrying.

"Dominique," he groaned when his mouth finally lifted from hers.

"Yes, yes, here," she concurred even as he was pushing her back against the tiles.

Oh, the glory of his flesh filling hers, lifting her up onto her toes, taking her mind and her soul with him.

"Charles," she choked out, her arms lifting to wind around his neck. "Kiss me some more."

He kissed her some more and made her whole, scattering her fears, taking her with him to that place where nothing existed but the two of them, together. Her heart sang with joy and her body thrummed with pleasure.

Charles loved her and she loved him. What more could she ever ask for?

CHAPTER EIGHT

HER real name was Jane Cooper, the report revealed, the only daughter of Scott and Tess Cooper, two seventeen-year-old teenagers who had run away from their small Tasmanian country town to live together in Hobart and who were never accepted back into either family fold. A magistrate had allowed them to marry when Tess became pregnant at eighteen.

Jane was born in Hobart but the young family of three soon moved to Keats Ridge on the west side of Tasmania, where her father worked for several years on the building of a nearby dam. Once the dam was built, however, employment opportunities dried up in the area and Keats Ridge was reduced to little more than a ghost town. The family lived on social security from the time Jane was eleven.

Charles frowned over this. Why didn't the man just move on to a place where there *was* work? What was wrong with him? Didn't he have any guts? Any goals? Any gumption?

Apparently not.

Charles's eyes dropped again to the report and he read on.

Jane's mother had never worked, except briefly as a waitress in a local tea shop. Although no photographs of her could be located by the investigator, locals said Tess Cooper was a very beautiful woman with lovely, long blonde hair and a great figure. They said the daughter, Jane, was the spitting image of her mother.

Jane attended the local primary school then the regional high school, where her attendance record was abysmal. She did pass her school certificate—just—but never completed her higher-school certificate. Her mother died when she was seventeen, the death certificate saying lung cancer. Locals remembered that Tess Cooper had been sick on and off for years. Rumour had it that her cancer had started elsewhere and finally spread to her lungs, which proved terminal. They said that towards the end Jane had left school permanently to nurse her mother, who died when she was just thirty-five and Jane seventeen. Scott Cooper, again according to the locals, had been a dead loss to his family, spending most days drinking at the one and only hotel still operating in town.

After her mother's death Jane moved to Launceston, where she worked in a fish and chip shop. At eighteen, she moved to the mainland, where she found work as a housemaid in a Melbourne hotel. Shortly thereafter, she changed her name to Dominique and started going to night school, doing secretarial and computer courses to begin with before later moving on to various sales and marketing diplomas.

Over the next six years she had worked her way

up in the hospitality industry, holding various clerical and guest-relations positions in Melbourne hotels before securing the job as PA to Jonathon Hall when she was twenty-six. That position had lasted two years.

Charles didn't need to read what had happened when she moved to Sydney. He knew that part.

The factual details of Dominique's childhood and working life were followed by edited transcripts of the taped interviews with various people of Dominique's past acquaintance, ten in all. Charles didn't have time to listen to the tapes just then—Dominique had said dinner would be ready in an hour—so he skimmed through the edited transcripts.

The first three interviews featured women who'd worked at the same hotels as Dominique during the years she was working on the reception desk in hotels. All described her as a clever but conniving creature with one aim in life. To become rich. They spoke of her flirting with the wealthier male guests, and probably sleeping with them—though when closely questioned they admitted this last was an assumption on their parts. They had no real evidence. Yes, Dominique had had boyfriends during the time they knew her, and they supplied a few names.

Four of these had been found and interviewed. All were working-class lads, all younger than Dominique. They all admitted to having been mad about her and all claimed they had slept with her.

One of them had said, ''It was love she didn't like.

The day after I told her I loved her, she broke up with me, said I was getting too serious. She said she was sorry, she liked me a lot but she didn't want to marry me."

Charles shook his head in dismay at reading this. Dominique's unfortunate background had elicited some sympathy and understanding from him. But how could you forgive anyone who used young men with such callousness? It was obvious that they were just research material in her quest to find out how to be good in bed. It amazed him that each of her so-called boyfriends held no bitterness towards her. All four said that they wished her well.

Her female colleagues, however, had shown absolutely no sympathy for her. The three of them had thought her a mercenary piece of work who only wanted one thing in life and made no bones about it. They all hoped she would be miserable.

It wasn't till Charles moved on to reading the first of the interviews with the three girls Dominique had flatted with in Melbourne—the first flatmate's name was Sandie—that he suspected jealousy might be influencing some of the women's views on Dominique. As he read on, he found it impossible to separate the truth from sheer malice.

Charles stopped reading at this juncture, deciding that maybe listening to the tone of this Sandie's voice would uncover the truth of the matter. Once he found the tape marked "Dominique's Melbourne flatmates", he swung round on his office chair and slotted it into the portable player he kept in the book shelves behind his desk. Changing the mode from CD to tape, he pressed play then settled back to listen.

It didn't take Charles long to see he'd been right. Talk about catty! Sandie was clearly relishing putting the knife in. She especially loved telling the investigator what Dominique had supposedly said about her next marital target being older, less handsome and more grateful than Hall.

"So what's happened?" she herself wanted to know. "Has Dominique seduced some rich old sucker up in Sydney and his family is all up in arms?"

Charles was grateful that the investigator had declined to answer.

The second flatmate, named Tricia, was even worse. Her comments were vicious. "Of course, females like her have ice in their veins, not blood. I've never met anyone more fake than Dominique Cooper. You only have to look at her hair and her boobs to know that. She was just one big fake!"

Charles winced, though not because either of those last accusations was true. Aside from his own upclose and personal knowledge of the subject, it was obvious from this report that Dominique had inherited her blonde hair and lovely figure from her mother. Her beauty was a matter of genes, not surgery, or a dye job.

Still, he could not discount the fact that a lot of what the two flatmates said was probably true, and his dismay increased.

"She took endless courses, you know," Tricia went on, her tone scathing. "Anything which would make her into a better man-trap. Deportment and grooming. Art and wine appreciation. Even cookery. When I asked her why she was doing a cookery course, she laughed and said that if sex didn't work, she might have to resort to food as the way to a man's heart. Well, perhaps she should have tried the cooking angle with Jonathon because obviously her fake brand of sex didn't do the trick. He dumped her in the end, didn't he? I have to confess I was never happier about anything in my whole life!"

Only one of the three flatmates interviewed proved to have more balanced views. Less black and white. Less condemning and more sympathetic. It was Claudia, Rico's cousin.

"You have to understand," Claudia said at one stage, "that Dominique was a damaged person. She confided in me one night that no one who hadn't lived her life could understand her attitude to money. It wasn't just that she'd been poor as a child. There was something about her mother's death which affected her greatly and which she hinted at but never explained. I gather her mother had been ill for a long time before she died. I don't think Dominique ever got over it."

Charles had no doubt this was the case. His own mother's death had been just as tragic in its own way and had affected him greatly. He could well imagine that nursing a terminally ill mother all those years under financially deprived circumstances could have twisted a young girl's mind. Dominique might have believed money would have saved her mother. Which it might very well have.

"I think she was a very sad girl underneath," Claudia went on to say, with considerable insight in Charles's opinion. "I felt sorry for her. She's not a bad person. I actually liked her a lot, but the other girls in the house hated her. Of course, they were just plain jealous. I mean…Dominique is simply stunning, isn't she? All their boyfriends tried to come on to her. Not that Dominique did anything to encourage them. She actually wasn't the flirty type. But heck, let's face it, she only had to walk into the room and all the men's mouths would drop open. Her body, I guess. Not to mention her hair, eyes, lips, legs, skin. I could go on and on but I'm sure you get my drift. Actually, I don't have much pity for this man she married. From what I gather he's filthy rich and not exactly a spring chicken. He probably only wanted a trophy wife on his arm and that gorgeous body in his bed. Rico told me he married her in no time flat, so what did he expect? The man should have got to know her first. But he didn't really want to get to know her, did he? He just wanted to get into her pants."

Charles flinched at this brutal statement. Because it was partly true. He hadn't bothered to really get to know Dominique. He'd never probed into her past. Maybe, subconsciously, he hadn't wanted to know.

He'd chosen to keep things superficial. He'd deceived himself, more than she had.

"She got what she wanted and he got what he wanted," Claudia pronounced with brutal frankness. "Sounds like a fair exchange to me. Marrying for love isn't what it's cracked up to be, anyway. I know. I've tried it and it sucked. Hey, I hope Dominique isn't going to hear any of this. Rico said she wouldn't. I would hate her to think she thought I didn't like her because I did. I would have liked to be her real friend, but she never let anyone get that close. She was afraid of love, I think. Yes, definitely afraid of it."

That's it! Charles realised, jumping to his feet. That explains everything. She was afraid of love, afraid to love him.

But she *did* love him. Why else would she have been crying when she came to him in the bathroom earlier? Why else would she worry that she wanted him too much?

Had he soothed her fears with his more tender love-making, first in the shower then back in bed? He seemed to have. She'd been like liquid in his arms afterwards, her skin all soft and glowing.

"Tell me you love me," she'd murmured as she'd gazed up into his eyes.

He was glad now that he had said he did, even if his motivation hadn't been clear at the time. He'd still been hedging his bets, not sure if he'd been going to hang in there with this marriage, or not.

Now he knew what he was going to do.

Charles clicked off the tape and pressed rewind on the tape deck. He was slipping the page of the report back with the other two tapes into the envelope when he heard Dominique's footsteps coming down the tiled hallway towards the den. He just had enough time to drop the envelope into the top drawer of his desk before she popped her head in the door.

"Can I come in or is the cloak and dagger bit still on?"

He tried to act naturally and not as if he was really seeing her for the first time. "All finished," he said.

"And?" She pushed open the door and moved further into the room.

Charles tried not to stare. Her blonde hair was swept up into a pony-tail and she was wearing a pale blue polar fleece track suit. Her face was free of make-up, except for some pink lipstick. She looked fresh and young and heart-stoppingly beautiful. All her earlier tears had vanished and she was smiling a warm and very relaxed smile.

"I take that back," she hurried on. "I don't want to know anything about that infernal report until you're happy to tell me. Did Rico ring? I didn't hear the phone."

"No. Not yet."

"Then why don't you ring him and get it over with? The last thing I want is that man interrupting our evening together."

"How long till dinner?"

"Around ten minutes or so."

"And what gourmet delights am I to look forward to?" he asked.

"Chicken and mushroom risotto followed by some decadent passion-fruit-topped cheesecake I found in the freezer, all washed down with that lovely bottle of Margaret River Chardonnay you had hiding at the back of the fridge. I know you prefer red but you can't possibly have red with risotto, Charles. I forbid it."

Charles did his best not to think negative thoughts about her wine and cooking skills, but it was difficult in the light of what he'd just heard.

"Rico would agree with you," he tossed off.

"Rico, Rico," she said irritably. "I'll never know what you see in that show-pony."

"Rico has depths you would never imagine."

"Rico? Don't make me laugh. Now, you have depth, Charles. Rico is all shadow and no substance. I'll bet he can't even cook!"

"You're wrong but I'm not going to argue with you."

"No, please don't. I'm far too happy tonight to argue with anyone. Now, don't be too long. Time's getting on and my poor little tummy's rumbling. You have fifteen minutes at most."

"I'll be with you in ten."

"I'll hold you to that."

Suddenly, she was gone, but her perfume lingered, as well as the memory of her wonderful smile. He could not dispute her claim of happiness. She had looked happy.

Had she decided she wasn't afraid to love him any longer? She'd said she loved him during their love-making in the shower and afterwards, back in bed. She'd told him over and over.

And he'd done the same. How could he not when his love for her welled up inside him all the time he was with her? The truth was he'd never been happier than since he'd met Dominique. What did it matter what forces had brought them together? Who cared if she'd been just after his money to begin with? He felt confident that her agenda had changed, that *she* had changed.

Of course, Rico would not believe a word of that. He would call it sentimental crap. He'd say Charles had been well and truly conned.

Charles didn't want to listen to Rico's arguments. Rico would learn the truth about Dominique eventually. By their tenth wedding anniversary he might even come to believe it.

Meanwhile, he would avoid any further discussions over Dominique for a while. He would let Rico think he was keeping her as his wife just till he got her out of his system. It was better than having to listen to his friend go on and on about how he should get rid of her all the time.

Charles reached for his phone and punched in Rico's number. No answer. He tried Rico's mobile and was about to hang up when the man himself answered in slurred tones.

Oh, dear. Rico only drank occasionally when he was upset over something.

"Charles here," Charles said with a sigh. "I see you didn't win at the races."

Rico laughed. "Actually, I did. Money-wise."

"So in what way *didn't* you win?"

"Let's just say the merry widow spoiled my day."

"How?"

"The usual way. God, but she's sarcastic."

"Did you know she was going to be there?"

His reluctance to answer confirmed what Charles already suspected.

"You did know," Charles said emphatically. "That's why you went. You're hung up on her, aren't you?"

"Don't be ridiculous! I can't stand her. She's everything I despise in a woman."

"Yes, I know," Charles said drily.

"Have you read the report?" Rico asked abruptly.

"Yes."

"And?"

"It looks damning."

"Too right it does. So what are you going to do about her?"

"Nothing. For now."

"I just knew you were going to say that. Be it on your head, then, Charles. You've been warned. Just remember. Revenge is a tricky path to take. You could end up getting even more hurt.''

"I appreciate your concern. And I appreciate the report. Sorry about going off at you last night. You were right to tell me." This way, his marriage now had a real chance of surviving. Because he was going to make a point of getting to know Dominique, and he would start by telling her more about himself. He would take her fully into his confidence about things he'd never told anyone, not even Rico. Then one day, when she was secure in his love, she might tell him all about herself.

"I wish someone had told me about Jasmine," Rico muttered. "*Before* the bloody wedding."

"You wouldn't have taken any notice. You were besotted."

"It's a failing I have, falling for the wrong type. No, forget I said that. I have not fallen for the merry widow. I'd just like to…"

"Get into her pants," Charles finished for him.

"Hell, no. I don't want her wearing pants. I don't want her wearing anything." He groaned. "Forget I said that, too. I've been drinking."

"So I noticed. I hope you're not driving anywhere later."

"Don't go big-brothering me, Charles. I can look after myself. For your information I'm in the foyer bar at the Regency, the one I took you to the other night. I came in a taxi and I won't be going home till tomorrow morning. Leanne will be here shortly."

Charles's eyebrows shot up. "Who's Leanne?"

"A very nice blonde I met the other night. Not unlike your Dominique to look at, except Leanne is already filthy rich. All she wants is my body. Which is a very nice change."

Charles sighed. "Renée was wrong the other night. Money *is* the root of all evil. But sex runs a close second."

"True. Otherwise you wouldn't be hanging on to that gold-digging wife of yours, pretending it's revenge. Talk about pathetic. I hope she's worth it, mate, because every day you keep her from now on is going to cost you. Chicks like that don't go quietly and the family law court judge you eventually front will wonder why you didn't get rid of her once you had that report in your hot little hands. You'll lose your best weapon if you continue to cohabit with the enemy. You do know that, don't you?"

"It's my life, Rico. I don't tell you what to do. Don't tell me."

"Right. Fine. Be a fool, then. See if I care." And he hung up.

Charles winced. Was he being a fool? Was Dominique still conning him?

No. No, he refused to believe that. She loved him, and he loved her. They just didn't know each other very well. Yet.

But time would remedy that. Starting tonight.

CHAPTER NINE

DOMINIQUE was proud of the table she'd set and the meal she'd cooked. That cookery course she'd once taken had finally come in useful. Up till now, she hadn't had the opportunity to cook for Charles, except at breakfast. And she'd hardly have needed to take an advanced cookery course in international cuisine to manage such simple fare. After all, she'd been cooking since she was thirteen.

"This looks marvellous, Dominique," Charles said. "Somehow I feel underdressed for the occasion."

"I like you in what you're wearing," she complimented as they sat down opposite each other on the glass table which fitted beautifully into the penthouse's hexagonal-shaped dining alcove. Three of the five walls enclosing them were glass through which you could see the city below, with its bright lights and busy streets. Saturday night was *the* night in Sydney, the many theatres and restaurants drawing lots of people.

"You have the right body for jeans," she went on. "Tall and lean, with long legs and a nice tight bottom. Yummy."

"Dominique! Really!"

"You're blushing," she said with a teasing laugh. "Are you deliberately trying to embarrass me?"

"Would I do that?" She laughed again. If Charles had one flaw, it was a tendency to be a bit stuffy occasionally. Though goodness knew he hadn't been stuffy the last day or so. Not in the bedroom, or out of it.

"I don't know," he replied.

She blinked, taken aback at the odd note in his voice. "What do you mean?"

He picked up his wine glass, which she'd already filled with the nicely chilled Margaret River Chardonnay. "I've been thinking how little we actually know about each other."

Dominique's whole body sucked in sharply, panic gripping her till she realised Charles hadn't meant anything sinister by it. He was sipping his wine and looking quite relaxed. Her automatic recoil at his remark, however, highlighted the fact that, no matter how happy and secure she felt in Charles's love, underneath she would always be worried that he might one day uncover the truth about her past. How could she ever explain the person she'd been before meeting him? Or the totally false family background she'd given him?

She couldn't. That was the truth of it. And the incessant worry.

Still, she at least had distance on her side. Charles would never be able to talk her into going back to Melbourne, or Tasmania. Never! And Charles himself was not a gadabout, or much of a traveller, even with his business interests. Like the intelligent man he was, he hired top people, then delegated. Recently, he admitted he hadn't been interstate in ages, despite Brandon Beer having a branch office in Melbourne. Now that he was married and about to become a family man, he would stay put in Sydney even more. The chance of his meeting anyone from her past who could paint her in an unflattering light was unlikely.

No, she was being paranoid again. All she had to do was keep to her original stories about her past and everything would be fine. Nothing would ever be achieved by confessing everything to him. He would simply never understand.

Even if he did travel to Melbourne, who was there after all who knew anything concrete? A few old workmates and flatmates whom she might have opened her foolish mouth to on occasion. Jonathon certainly wasn't a danger. No way would he talk about her in a derogatory way. He'd been the guilty one at the end of that relationship, not her.

Besides, Charles already knew all about him. She'd pretty well told the truth about Jonathon, except for the inference that she'd been in love with the man. She'd had to do that or end up sounding like a tramp.

In fairness to herself, she'd been very seriously attracted to Jonathon. She'd admired his energy and ambition, and had even enjoyed sleeping with him. Up to a point. That had been somewhat of a shock, since he was a very experienced lover, much more so than the boys she'd known before him.

Dear God, it had been a long time since she'd thought about those early boyfriends. Had she hurt them? She hoped not. They'd all been very sweet, and very nice to her, unlike the people she'd been working with at the time. She hadn't been totally callous. Each one had been her friend as well. And everyone needed a friend sometimes. She couldn't seem to make close girlfriends the way other girls did. Other women always found her looks threatening.

"You're not eating your dinner," Charles said, breaking into her thoughts. "And it's delicious. I can see I'm going to enjoy coming home to this every night."

"What? Oh, yes, that's nice." Dominique had to force herself to blot out those infernal worries about her past and concentrate on the present. She'd wiped the slate clean when she'd met and fallen in love with Charles. Now her priority had to be her husband, and their future together. This constant worrying over things she could not change was a waste of time.

A warm smile crossed her mouth with this sensible resolve. "I'm glad you like it. And the wine?"

"Perfect. I will defer to your excellent judgement on such matters in future."

"Now, now, don't start patronising me again, Charles," she said, but with a smile on her lips. "I know you know heaps about wine and food and all things cultured. I'm just a philistine by comparison.

But that's all right. You can teach me all the things I don't know.''

''My pleasure,'' he murmured, and smiled over the table at her.

Dominique's stomach curled over. There it was again, that new and quite wicked gleam in his eyes. suddenly, she was fiercely aware of her braless breasts underneath her clothes, her naked nipples peaking hard against the fleecy-lined material.

This was another of her concerns, this…this change in Charles, plus her own avid willingness to accommodate whatever he had in mind. The memory of his tender and reassuring lovemaking in bed less than two hours ago receded in her mind, replaced by the stirring of an excitement over what he might want later this evening.

Sex with Charles had always been unlike any she'd ever experienced before. Everything was more intensified. As a lover, Charles was by far the best she'd ever had. He could make her melt with a single kiss.

But Charles in this new rakish mode seduced her mind as well as her body. Once he'd set his eyes on her the way he had at this very moment, she had difficulty thinking of anything else but what he was going to do to her after this meal was over.

If they lasted that long, that was…

Suddenly, she was sitting there like a cat on a hot tin roof, her appetite for food gone. She picked up her wine glass and took a deep swallow, then another, knowing that wine sometimes stimulated her appetite and relaxed her at the same time. She desperately needed both.

Fortunately, Charles dropped his eyes and resumed eating the risotto with irritating gusto. Wasn't it just like a man, she thought irritably, that nothing stopped him from eating? Dominique finally picked up her fork again, though not with much enthusiasm. Her mind was still on other things.

"Not hungry?" he asked on glancing up after clearing his plate and seeing that she was only toying with her food.

"I'm saving some room for dessert," she lied. "Cheesecakes are a weakness with me."

Abruptly, she stood up, and was about to whisk away both the plates from the table when he asked her to sit down again.

"What's wrong?" she asked, that now familiar panic churning away in her stomach.

"Just sit down again, please, Dominique," he repeated.

Charles watched her worried eyes as she sank back down into her chair. He'd originally been going to wait till after dessert before trying to get Dominique to exchange confidences about the past. Such a touchy project required a degree of subtlety and finesse, and he'd been hoping that by then the food and wine would have disarmed her.

But she'd hardly eaten any risotto or drunk more than two mouthfuls of the wine.

"I have a confession to make."

"Oh?" Her lovely pink lips pulled back into a shaky smile. "What have you done? Don't tell me you've been having an affair with the merry widow all along."

Charles's head snapped back in surprise. "Goodness, no. No, whatever would make you even think such a thing?"

"You've never slept with her, even before me?" she persisted.

"No," he stated firmly, despite feeling pleased over her jealousy. Gold-digging wives wouldn't be jealous of their husbands. Why should they be when they didn't really love?

"Good," she said. "I don't think I could have stood that, especially with you playing poker with her every Friday night. So what other dreadful thing have you done?"

"Nothing dreadful. But I didn't tell you the total truth about my mother's death."

Her mouth dropped open. "She...she didn't die from kidney failure?"

"She did, but only because of the cocktail of sleeping tablets and whisky which she'd swallowed the night before."

"Charles! Oh, my God...oh, how awful for you!"

How perverse, Charles thought as his heart twisted. He'd honestly believed he was over his mother's suicide.

Apparently not.

But of course, now that he thought about it, why

would he keep her suicide a deep, dark secret if he was over it? He wasn't much different from Dominique, really, hugging the skeletons in his family's closet to himself. He'd told her the truth about his father's death—he'd fallen onto a crevasse whilst skiing on a New Zealand mountainside—but he'd never said a word about the man's profligate ways, or his mother's ongoing depression over the state of her marriage.

"Yes," he agreed, and picked up his glass of wine. "Yes, it was awful."

"Would you like to talk about it?" Dominique asked gently.

He looked deep into her sympathetic eyes as he sipped some more of the wine.

"You don't have to if you don't want to," she added, her eyes soft and kind. "I would understand if you don't."

He found it tellingly difficult but he told her. The whole, awful truth. His mother was an abused wife. Not physically, but emotionally. His father had only married her because she'd been pregnant with him and his own father had threatened to disinherit him if he didn't.

Jason Brandon had not been good husband and father material. He'd been a womaniser and a wastrel. He'd been left a healthy company when his own father passed away, but by the time Jason Brandon died in his late forties Brandon Beer had been close to bankruptcy.

At that time Charles had been at university, living on campus, happy to be anywhere but at home. It had been just twelve months since his mother's supposedly accidental death and Charles wanted nothing more to do with his father. It wasn't till he was going through his father's private desk the night after the man's own funeral that Charles had found his mother's last diary—she'd always kept one—detailing her escalating depression and despair, and the reasons behind her suicide. Apparently, his father had become addicted to call girls during his forties and would often have them visit the house to entertain him all night whilst his mother, poor, weak woman that she was, was banished to the guest room.

Discovering that his father was utterly amoral and cruel besides being lazy and incompetent had come as a great shock to Charles. Shocking too was the added revelation that the reason his mother had never had any more children after Charles was born was because his father refused to sleep with her after their wedding night. According to the poor woman's diary, he had denounced his bride the morning after their wedding night as disgustingly ugly and utterly boring in bed, crushing her self-esteem and shattering her illusion that he really loved her.

After that their marriage had been just a charade, with his mother putting on a brave face for the sake of her son, and his supposed inheritance.

Charles admitted to Dominique that he'd been kept in ignorance of his parents' marital problems all his life, being sent away from home a lot, first to boarding-school, then to summer camps during the school holidays, then finally to live on the university campus. He'd never got to know his father at all on a personal basis and he knew little more of his mother, although he knew she was unhappy.

"Why Dad kept that damning diary, I will never know," he ground out. "Maybe he liked looking at it. Maybe he liked reading about his exploits through my poor mother's tormented eyes."

"Oh, surely not, Charles. Surely no one could be that wicked."

"He *was* wicked. I hate to think I carry his genes. I sometimes take comfort from the fact I don't look like him."

"Maybe you take after your grandfather. He sounds as if he was a hard-working man."

"Yes, he was. A good man, too. Who knows why my father turned out the way he did? So which of your parents do you think you take after?" Charles asked, hoping that his confession and confidences might inspire Dominique to offer the same.

The kindness in her eyes clouded to a bleak unhappiness. "I...I don't like talking about my parents, Charles."

"Why's that? Because they were killed so tragically?"

"No. Because they're the past. I hate the past. At least, I hate the past before I married you. I like to think of our wedding day as the first day of my new life. All that went before wasn't worth remembering.''

''Your mother wasn't worth remembering?'' Charles probed gently. ''That's an odd thing for a daughter to say.''

Her eyes showed agitation. ''Please, Charles, can we talk about something else?''

Charles sighed. So much for his idea of exchanging confidences. Clearly, it was too soon. Still...

''The last thing I want to do is upset you,'' he said. ''It's just that I've been thinking how little we really know about each other. I mean...I know your taste in things like food and wine and books and movies. I know you're a hard worker and a perfectionist when it comes to your appearance. I know you like pale colours and you don't like men who swear. I know you're intelligent and good in bed. But I don't know what makes you tick, down deep.''

Charles leant back in his chair, holding her eyes with his. ''Who and what we are usually comes from our childhood. And from our parents. My mother was a sensitive but weak woman. I grew up thinking I was sensitive and weak too, mainly because my father kept telling me I was. It wasn't till my mother died that I stopped believing anything *he* said. He didn't even have the decency to grieve. After the liberation of *his* death, my real self started to come to the fore. To my surprise I had many hidden strengths, a tunnel-vision drive and limitless ambition. Sure, I was still sensitive in some areas. I hadn't inherited my father's looks or charm, you see, so my early encounters with the opposite sex were not a raging success.''

''I find that hard to believe!'' Dominique broke in, her expression genuinely startled. ''You're just being extra-modest for some reason.''

''See? You don't know me as well as you might think you do.''

''I know you're a marvellous lover. And you *are* good-looking. At least, you are in my eyes. Everyone has a different opinion over what good-looking is, Charles. You have the sexiest eyes, do you know that?''

He didn't. But he could almost believe it when she looked at him the way she was looking at him at this moment. As his flesh stirred Charles gave up the idea of coaxing the truth out of Dominique tonight. It probably *was* too soon, anyway. She needed more time to trust him with such sensitive information. It wasn't every day that a wife would readily confess to her husband that she'd been a gold-digger before she met him. She might *never* admit it.

Meanwhile, tonight's agenda had changed.

''Why don't we skip dessert for now, take this bottle of wine with us and go skinny dipping in the pool?'' he suggested.

Her eyes gleamed at the idea, then darkened momentarily. ''But do we have total privacy out there?'' she asked. ''Are you sure no one will see us? I mean…aren't some of the nearby buildings taller than this one?''

"Yes, but they're office blocks. No one will be working this hour on a Saturday night."

"How do you know?"

How odd, Charles thought, that her reluctance to go along with his idea was now annoying him. He should have been pleased. Instead, he felt nothing but frustration.

"Well, if there are some idiots working back, then they'd have to be serious workaholics and will hardly be peering out of windows. You can wear a costume if you want," he said. "But I'm not."

"You've become quite wicked just lately, do you know that?" she said, her voice a mixture of excitement and exasperation. "You know I won't be able to resist. You *know* it, you devil!"

Yes, he realised with a rush of dark triumph. He did. But he still wasn't absolutely sure of her; still couldn't quite dismiss all that he'd read in that rotten report.

He wouldn't be sure of her till everything was out in the open, something which might never happen. Meanwhile, he had to content himself with the satisfaction of seeing her as helplessly turned on as she was at this moment.

Oh, yes, she couldn't hide her aroused state. The evidence of her desire was there for him to see, in her glittering blue eyes and fiercely erect nipples. Her need for him would overwhelm any qualms over their being seen. His own need would do the same.

Just thinking about it sent hot blood charging

through his veins, swelling his pained flesh even further. He would not take no for an answer this time. She would do what he wanted, where he wanted. She would be his, tonight and forever. To hell with the past. To hell with everything but being with Dominique. His wife. His love. His torment!

CHAPTER TEN

"If you like it so much, it's yours."

Dominique whirled from where she'd been practically drooling over the all-white kitchen, her eyes wide with surprise. As much as she liked everything about the house, not just the kitchen, Charles had seemed unimpressed.

"You mean it? Even though you'll have to cross the bridge to go to work?"

"I'll tolerate the inconvenience."

They'd looked at house after house in the eastern suburbs all morning and nothing had taken Dominique's eye. The homes had either been too large or too small. After lunch in a city café, Charles had suggested a change in real-estate agencies. This time, a lady had come to their aid.

Her name was Coral, she was in her forties and had the brains to be more interested in what the wife had in mind, rather than the husband. The first thing she did before launching them back on to the inspection road was ask Dominique to describe her perfect house.

Dominique rattled off her requirements from the list in her head. At least four bedrooms, with the master bedroom having walk-in wardrobes and a spacious *en suite*; a study for Charles and formal lounge and dining areas for entertaining. Critical was a large family room and an equally large kitchen which overlooked a garden with a safely enclosed solar-heated pool and some room left over for children to play in, plus at least a two-car garage with some off-street parking room for visitors. Dominique added that architecturally and décor-wise, she preferred clean, simple lines, tall ceilings, lots of windows, no stairs and no bright colours. Oh, and air-conditioning, if possible.

When asked if she wanted a harbour view, Dominique declined the idea. As much as it sounded very nice, she noticed from viewing various harbourside homes that their back gardens and water-facing balconies were invariably windswept and cold. Maybe they'd be fine to live in in the summer, but she was after a functional family home which would be comfortable all year round.

She'd thought it was a tall order but Coral brought her straight to this property at Clifton Gardens—a suburb not far north of the bridge—and *voilà*, it was as though a genie had conjured the place up from what Dominique had described. Everything was there. Absolutely everything, including air-conditioning. Even the outside of the single-storey residence found favour, being cement-rendered and painted cream with a black trim around the windows and guttering. Classy and elegant-looking.

Better still, it was empty with the owner keen to

settle as soon as possible. He was a television anchor man and had recently taken a job in Hong Kong. He and his family had only been gone a few days and the place still had a nice, clean, lived-in smell about it. A happy feel, too.

Dominique was surprised when this thought popped into her head. She did not believe in ghosts, or superstitions, or atmospheres. She'd always been a pragmatic and very practical person. Houses didn't have souls—or give off auras—in her opinion.

Yet this house felt just right.

And she said as much to Charles.

He smiled at her. "If you say so, Goldilocks."

"Goldilocks?"

"Yes. That house was too large," he mimicked in a little-girl voice. "And that other house was too small. But this house is *just* right."

Dominique laughed and so did Coral.

"Your husband has a sense of humour," she said.

"Her husband is sick of house-hunting already," Charles said drily. "Can we go home now, if I promise to put a deposit on this place first thing tomorrow morning?"

Dominique tried not to get too excited too soon. "But you haven't even asked how much it is."

"How much is it?" he asked Coral.

"Er—the owners are looking for two-point-five million."

Dominique was staggered whilst Charles remained cool. "Is it worth it?" he asked.

"Every cent," the real-estate agent replied confidently. "It's a very big block of land and a top position. But I'd still only offer them two mil to start with. They're very keen to sell quickly."

"No. No offers. No haggling. I'll pay the full sum. Here's my card."

Coral stared down at it, then up at him. "You're Charles Brandon, of Brandon Beer."

"That's right."

"I didn't recognise you. Silly me. Oh, wow!"

"Wow what?"

"Wow, I'm going to come first in commission this month because you're really going to buy this place, aren't you?"

"Sure am, Coral. My solicitor will be in touch first thing in the morning. Now, if you'll excuse me, it's been a long day so far and I'd like to go home."

"I know what you'd like," Dominique whispered as he shepherded her towards the still open front door.

"I have no idea what you mean," he returned smoothly, but the corner of his mouth lifted in a devilish smirk.

Dominique broke out into goose-pimples. For this man, no time was the wrong time, no place sacrosanct against his escalating desires. He wanted her in all sorts of places and all sorts of ways. Out in the pool last night for instance. Now, *that* had been one wild experience.

Dominique shivered at the memory. As exciting as

it had been, she'd felt embarrassed afterwards. Never again, she vowed.

She was about to tell Charles that making love in the pool was not on when a sound distracted her, a piteous meow, coming from somewhere above their heads. They'd come through the front door and had just stepped down onto the curving front path which wound its stylish way through the almost maintenance-free Japanese-style garden.

Dominique spun round and looked up. There, on the roof, was a slender, reddish-brown cat with slightly oversized ears and the sweetest little face.

"Oh, look, Charles, it's a cat!"

Charles rolled his eyes at her. "Yes," he said in droll tones. "I do believe it is. Come on. Let's go."

She pulled away from his urging grip and stood her ground. "But it looks hungry and lost."

"Dominique, I doubt that very much. It has a collar and tag around its neck."

The cat meowed piteously again and Dominique decided to go with her gut instinct and ignore Charles's quite logical observation. "No, she's in some kind of trouble and I'm going to help her. She probably can't get down from the roof and has been up there for days. She's very thin."

"What makes you think it's a she? It could be a he."

"With that face? No, it's a girl cat. I'm sure of it."

"Come to think of it, so am I. A boy cat would have more sense."

"Did I hear you say there was a cat on the roof?" Coral said as she joined them outside.

"Yes. Up there. Look." Dominique pointed to where the cat was peering plaintively down at them over the black guttering. Clearly, she wanted to get down but was wary of doing so.

"Goodness, that's the owners' old cat. We've met several times before. Her name's Rusty. She's part-Abyssinian."

"In that case, what's she doing still here, all alone?" Dominique said, distressed. "Oh, no, they just left her behind, didn't they?"

"I don't think they would do anything like that. The Jenkinses are very nice people. The day before they left, they gave Rusty to some friends of theirs in Newport because they couldn't take pets with them to Hong Kong. The apartment block they'll be living in doesn't allow it. I'll bet the poor old thing's run away and come home. She's not young—I think she's eight or nine—and this is the only home she's ever known." Coral sighed. "I'll have to ring the Jenkinses in Hong Kong and find out the name and number of their friends and organise for them to come and get her."

"But that won't work," Dominique said agitatedly. "She'll just run away again. Next time, she might not make it back here in one piece. Newport is miles away! She might get run over or attacked by a stray dog!" Dominique saw in a flash what she had to do. "We'll take her home with us," she announced. "I'll keep her inside till we move in here. Then she can live out the rest of her years in the home she knows and obviously loves.''

"Hey, hold it there!'' Charles protested. "You can't do that. We're not supposed to have pets in our building, either.''

"Oh, phooey. We can smuggle her in. And it's not for very long. Only a few weeks at most. Didn't you say the owners wanted to settle this sale quickly, Coral?''

"Yes, indeed. That's a wonderful idea, Dominique. And so very good of you. I know Mrs Jenkins will be relieved. She was very upset at having to leave Rusty behind. I don't think *Mr* Jenkins understood her feelings at all.''

"Some men can be very insensitive,'' Dominique agreed. "Not many of them are like my darling husband,'' she added, batting coy eyelashes up at Charles as she linked arms with him and drew him close to her side. "Agree with everything I say, Charlie-boy,'' she whispered under her breath, "or there'll be no hanky-panky for you when we get home.''

Charles smiled, but whether from amusement or necessity he wasn't sure. The boot was definitely on the other foot for the moment. She had him jumping through her hoops, not the other way around as it had been last night. Hell, he shouldn't have thought about that. Talk about wicked.

"Now, up you go, darling,'' she was saying. "And get Rusty down for us.''

He turned disbelieving eyes her way. "You want me to climb up on that roof?"

She batted those baby blues up at him. "Uh-huh."

"How?" he demanded to know. "The place is empty. No ladders in the garage, or anything else, if I recall. I'm not a superhero, you know. I can't fly."

"You'll find a way," she said. "You're a very inventive man." And her eyes sparkled mischievously at him.

It was at that point Charles gave up and surrendered himself totally to this woman he'd married. Strangely, it was an extremely liberating experience, accepting the fact that he would always love her, no matter what. But it was the choosing to believe that she really loved him back which brought the most surprising peace of mind.

Suddenly, all those lingering doubts and fears which had been niggling away at him were gone, as well as the need to keep testing her in various ways.

"Right," he said, and went in search of whatever he could find to help his rescue mission. The wheely bin around the side of the house was just the thing. Once manoeuvred into position over the garages— that was where the guttering was at its lowest—he hauled himself up onto the roof quite easily. Just as well he was wearing jeans, however, and fairly fit. It took an extra minute or two to gain the cat's confidence, but eventually, with a few soft words and the odd stroke or two, Rusty eventually let him lift her up and lower her gently into Dominique's waiting arms.

The way his wife looked up at him at that moment moved Charles more than the way she looked at him when they were making love.

"Thank you," was all she said, but those two simple words said *I love you* better than any impassioned declaration of love ever could.

By the time he'd made it safely down again, the cat had snuggled into Dominique's arms as if it had been there all its life.

"Oh, isn't she a darling, Charles?" Dominique said when Rusty started to purr.

"Yes," he said, but he was looking at her, not the cat.

"We'll have to go shopping for some house-cat things," she said happily. "She'll need a couple of kitty litter trays. We wouldn't want her not to be able to find one when she needed it. And a bed. One of those raised trampoline styles are best, I'm told. And some bowls for food and water. And some food, of course. Oh, and we'll have to find a vet tomorrow, Charles. Have her checked over. Coral, could you ring me later tonight with Mrs Jenkins's phone number in Hong Kong? I'll give her a ring and find out what Rusty likes."

Charles shook his head whilst Coral nodded. "I'll do that. You have a good woman there, Mr Brandon. Very kind. Not many people would bother."

No, he realised. Not many would.

"I'm not being kind," Dominique denied. "I'm being totally selfish. I've always wanted a cat but I've never had one.

"You don't mind, do you, Charles?" she asked him once they were back in his car, and alone. By then the obviously very tired cat was almost asleep in her lap.

He smiled over at her. "No. Of course not. You have whatever you want."

She gazed at the house again through the passenger window. "I can't tell you how much it means to me, Charles, to have a house like that to raise my children in. If you saw the shack I lived in as a child... No, no, I don't want to think about that. That's dead and gone."

She reached over to touch him on his arm, her eyes lifting to lock with his. "I am *so* lucky to have found a man like you."

He leant over and kissed her softly on the lips. "I think I'm the lucky one in this car."

Charles was alarmed to find tears in her eyes when his head lifted.

"I...I do love you, Charles," she said in a tone which betrayed doubt in his belief of that fact.

"I know," he returned warmly. "And I love you. Now let's go home."

He was glad to turn his attention to driving the car. Tears always made him feel uncomfortable. His mother had cried a lot.

"We're going to be very happy in that house, you know. It's a happy house."

"A *happy* house? That's an odd thing to say. What makes it a happy house?"

"It's just a feeling I got when I walked in. Maybe that's why Rusty came back. Because she felt it too."

Charles smiled. "I didn't realise you were such a sentimentalist."

"I'm not. Not usually. But I think I'm in danger of becoming one since marrying you."

"That's sweet. There again, you are sweet."

"No one has ever thought so before," she said with a sigh as she continued to stroke the cat in her lap.

"Not true. Coral thought so."

"That's a first, believe me. Women usually can't stand me."

"I would imagine a less mature woman might be jealous of your looks. But I can assure you that Renée likes you. She called you a lovely girl the other night at poker."

Charles was touched by the look of surprise on his wife's face.

"Did she *really*?"

"Absolutely." It wasn't really a lie, although Charles was pretty sure Renée had been talking about Dominique's beauty.

"I...I'd like to become better friends with her," Dominique said. "But she's a bit...formidable, isn't she?"

Charles laughed. "I know what you mean. The

merry widow doesn't suffer fools gladly. She gives poor Rico a hard time.''

''Pardon me if I don't feel sorry for *poor* Rico.''

Charles knew where Dominique was coming from. He really had to straighten Rico out where his wife was concerned; had to make him see that she hadn't married him just for his money.

He wasn't stupid enough not to think his money added to his attractions, or that Dominique would ever have married a poor man. But that was a far cry from believing her a cold-blooded gold-digger. She obviously had complex issues where money was concerned, and a deep-rooted sense of insecurity.

''Charles...''

''What now?''

''You're going the wrong way. I doubt there are any pet shops open in the city on a Sunday. We'll have to find a shopping mall in the suburbs.''

Charles swore, at which Dominique placed her hands over Rusty's ears. ''Not in front of the cat, dear.''

He groaned. ''I think I'm going to regret letting you have that damned cat.''

''No, you won't. Because it's made me love you all the more.''

''Just because I let you have a cat?''

''Yes.'' She sighed an almost weary sigh. ''When I was about fourteen, this bedraggled kitten wandered into our back yard and cried and cried at our back door. When I went to give it some milk my father yelled at me not to, then shooed the cat away. He said we couldn't afford to feed it. But we could afford his going down to the pub every day, couldn't we?'' she added bitingly.

Charles didn't know what to say. Best perhaps not to say a thing, he decided. Best to just let her talk.

''He was a drunk. A pathetic drunk. And I really don't want to talk about him any more. Even thinking about my father is enough to put me in a bad mood. And I don't want to be in a bad mood today. Today, I'm happy and I'm going to go on being happy. Please don't ask me any more about him, Charles.''

''All right,'' he said gently. He wished she'd told him more but even the little she had said was important. Bit by bit the pieces of the puzzle which was his wife were coming together.

What hell she must have gone through as a child, with her mother dying a slow, painful death and her father obviously being a hopeless alcoholic.

Dominique would no doubt be shocked to learn how her father had turned his life around during the past decade. Though shocked might not be the word. Charles suspected she'd be furious. She would not understand why he couldn't have done that when she and her mother had needed him.

No, she would not be pleased at that little piece of news. Still, she was unlikely to ever find out. Charles couldn't see her ever going in search of her father again, and *he* had no intention of telling her. How could he ever explain how he knew?

No, he could never reveal anything he'd found out from that report. And he'd have to make sure Rico never did, either.

Rico…

Now, Rico could present a bit of a problem. He really had it in for Dominique. Fortunately, their paths wouldn't cross this week, but come next Friday night he would tell Rico straight that his marriage was a goer, he'd advise him that he'd bought a house and was going ahead with the baby idea, and he was to change his attitude towards Dominique, or else!

Or else what? Charles pondered.

Was he prepared to give up his friendship with Rico for Dominique? Maybe even his Friday-night poker game altogether? His partnerships in the race-horses he shared with the man?

Yes, he realised. Such was the measure of his love for his wife, and his faith in her. She had to come first with him. Today, tomorrow and forever!

CHAPTER ELEVEN

"I CAN'T believe it's only a week since you last went to play poker," Dominique said as she watched Charles get dressed. "It seems so much longer."

Charles smiled a wry smile. "I can see it's time for me to go back to work. Time always goes slowly when you're in boring company."

Charles rather liked seeing the shock his self-deprecating remark brought to her beautiful face.

"Don't be ridiculous, Charles. You know that's not what I meant. It's just that it's been such a full week, what with deciding on the house and looking at furniture and…"

"And playing mother to that infernal cat I was weak enough to let you keep," he finished for her, his eyes flicking ruefully at the bundle of contented fur curled up next to her on the bed.

So much for his edict the first night that the cat was banned from their bedroom. One little meow at the door and Dominique had been up like a flash. Of course, once Rusty's newly purchased trampoline bed—the deluxe model complete with built-in heat pad—had been brought into their room, all the meowing had miraculously ceased.

Within twenty-four hours of the cat's arrival, Rusty

had the run of the whole penthouse, with Dominique her devoted slave. Nothing was too much trouble for her darling puss.

Not that Charles really minded. He rather liked seeing Dominique's maternal side. She was going to make a marvellous mother. And, to be truthful, Rusty was actually an independent old dear and not much trouble after that first night. By Tuesday, the cat didn't care where she slept, as long as it was warm and comfortable. During the day, she would find herself a sunny spot on the carpet, curl up and go to sleep. The lounge chair closest to the TV was her favourite spot at night. She seemed to genuinely enjoy watching the television.

Charles happily left the television on all night for her so that he didn't have those curious cat's eyes on him whilst he was making love to Dominique. Bad enough that their bedrooom activities had been curtailed somewhat during the day, not so much because of the cat's presence but because Dominique had become obsessed with her plans for the house. She spent hours on the internet, looking at furniture and furnishings and other home-wares. Charles had perhaps foolishly given her a blank cheque over the decorating, which she wanted to do herself, and she was taking the job very seriously.

By mid-week, he'd begun to feel more jealous of that darned house than the cat. By today, he'd been so frustrated he'd pounced on Dominique mid-afternoon and thrown her across his desk for some very hot lovemaking. She'd been a bit stunned by the speed of things but no less enthusiastic than usual.

"So what are you going to do whilst I'm gone?" he asked as he slipped his wallet and keys into his trouser pocket.

"Oh, just woman things. My hair could do with a moisture treatment and my nails badly need redoing. But first, I'm going to run myself a big bubble bath and just relax for an hour or two. Pamper myself. By the time you get home, I'm going to be all gorgeous and glowing."

"You're always gorgeous and glowing in my eyes," he said, bending to kiss the top her head.

"You're just saying that so that I'll forgive you for attacking me in your study this afternoon."

He laughed. "I didn't hear you saying no."

"You were too fast for me to say anything!"

"Not too fast for you not to enjoy it, I noticed."

Her blush was endearing.

"I still don't know how you do that."

"How I do what?"

"Charles Brandon, stop being such an egotist! You know exactly what I mean."

"Why worry about it? Just lie back and have a good time."

"Huh. Hard to lie back and seriously have a good time when you've got Biros and things sticking into your backside. Next time, clear the top of your desk first."

"With pleasure. And the first thing to go will be that infernal computer."

"Don't you dare. I *love* that computer."

"What you love is the online shopping! You're never off the darned thing."

"I know. I have been rather obsessive about it this week, haven't I? How about I promise not to go on the internet even once over the weekend? I'll leave all that till you go back to work on Monday."

"Cross your heart and hope to die?"

"Absolutely." And she made the gesture.

"Great. I'll look forward to it."

"But you have to promise to take me out as well."

"As well as what?" he asked, feigning an innocent look.

She pulled a face at him. "I hope you bluff better than that tonight at poker."

"I happen to be a superb bluffer."

She chortled. "You lost last week, if I recall."

"Tonight is another night entirely. I'm going to be right on my game tonight."

"That's what you said last Friday night when you knocked me back in this very room. If you lose again tonight, try not to go too primitive on me when you get home."

"What? Oh, yes," he said, guilt rushing in as he recalled what had happened the previous Friday night. Thank heavens she'd never find out what had been going through his mind at the time. "Right. I promise. Better go. Don't want to be late."

"Heaven forbid."

Dominique watched him hurry off. What was the attraction with that game? she wondered. She'd never liked cards herself, let alone playing them for money. There again, gambling in any form was not something she'd ever do. She'd always hated the idea of risking her hard-earned money. Still, Charles obviously enjoyed it.

There again, he probably considered playing poker more entertainment than gambling. She doubted he was seriously trying to win money when he played cards, or placed a bet on one of his racehorses. He was already fabulously wealthy. Winning and losing would be more a question of ego with him, rather than money. Charles was very competitive, as all successful businessmen were.

Dominique rose from the bed, leaving Rusty to sleep. She made her way into the bathroom, humming happily as she went about turning on the taps and pouring in the scented bubble bath. She was really looking forward to lying back in the water and listening to some of her favourite music.

What a change from her mood the previous Friday night, when she'd been worried sick about Charles playing poker with the merry widow. Amazing, really, what a difference this past week had made. She'd never felt happier, or more confident in the future. Charles really loved her and Renée was no longer a threat in her mind.

Then there was that wonderful house Charles had

bought, and her lovely cat. All she needed now to make her life perfect was a baby.

This last thought brought a frown. She really didn't want to keep taking that Pill for another cycle. For who knew how long it might take her to get pregnant? Just wanting a baby did not always produce one.

She'd read it was more a matter of timing and abstaining till the time was right. Too much sex and the male sperm count went down, according to the article she'd read at a hairdressing salon the week before her wedding. By then, she'd been drawn to articles like that.

With a sigh, Dominique realised Charles would not be happy about abstaining just yet. Hopefully, he'd get over it once he went back to work next week. Maybe she could help by giving him more lovemaking than he could handle this weekend, starting with when he arrived home tonight.

Dominique smiled at the deviousness of her plan. By Monday Charles would be running to the office for a rest and more than willing to go along with her going off the Pill and trying for a baby next month!

Just the thought of having their baby put her on a high. And to think that seven days ago she'd been worried that something might go wrong; that her loving Charles as much as she did was a sure recipe for disaster.

Falling in love with Charles, she realised, was the best thing that had ever happened to her. Even though she hadn't appreciated it at the time. The

Dominique she'd been back then could not handle love. She'd reacted with panic and fear. Even as recently as last week, she'd still been afraid. Now she had finally accepted that love did not necessarily equate with weakness and foolishness. Love—and being loved back—could be wonderful and warm and the most secure feeling in the world.

Rico was the only potential fly left in the ointment, and he too didn't seem to be such a problem any more. Charles hadn't even rung the man all week. Maybe he'd decided to cool their friendship somewhat, now that he was a married man, and soon to become a family man. Maybe he was as sick of the Italian playboy's cynicism as she was.

Whatever, Dominique wasn't going to think about Rico tonight. Nothing was going to spoil her good mood, or the prospect of a lovely, quiet evening pampering herself to the greatest degree before she launched into Project Love Overload!

Once the bubble bath was ready, Dominique collected a couple of her favourite CDs from Charles's huge collection in the living room. Then she went along to his study to get the portable CD player she'd noticed he kept in his bookcase behind the desk. With that in hand, Dominique returned to the bathroom, where she positioned the player on the shelf above the corner of the spa bath and plugged it into a nearby power point. Slotting the first CD into the player, Dominique stripped off and slowly climbed into the steamingly fragrant water. It wasn't till she'd lowered herself beneath the frothy bubbles that she realised she hadn't pressed play.

With a groan, she peered up over her head and decided she could just reach the play button on the side without fully getting out again. It was a stretch but she made it, unaware that the button she pressed was not the CD-play button but the cassette-play button. Not many people used tapes any more and it hadn't occurred to Dominique that the player even had a tape section or that it would be set on to tape. When a male voice echoed through the bathroom, her first reaction was surprise. But surprise quickly gave way to shock when her name was mentioned, and a woman started talking.

"Sandie?" Dominique gasped, and sat bolt upright in the bath, her head spinning as she tried to work out why Charles would have a tape with her Melbourne flatmate talking on it.

There was no doubt in Dominique's mind that it was Sandie. Her voice was quite distinctive with its abrasive delivery and nasal whine. But the things she was saying, and all about her!

Dominique had always known Sandie didn't like her, especially after Sandie's boyfriend had made a rude suggestion to her and Dominique had complained about it. But this wasn't dislike she was hearing. This was hatred, and condemnation, and contempt.

Tricia followed, with more damning opinions, all branding her a heartless fortune hunter.

The trouble was Dominique could not deny the basic truths of what they were saying. Behind the hostility and viciousness lay fact, not fiction. She had been everything they accused her of being. Heartless. Mercenary. Ruthless.

Dominique sat there, frozen, in the bath, yet her heart was going like a jack-hammer inside her chest.

''Oh, God,'' she kept saying over and over.

The realisation that Charles must have had her investigated at some stage both appalled and bewildered Dominique. The blood began pounding in her temples and she could hardly think. Shock was scrambling her normally sharp brains and she struggled to make sense of it all.

If he'd known all this, then why had he still married her?

It wasn't till the tape rolled on to the interview with Claudia—the third of Dominique's Melbourne flatmates—and the girl mentioned Rico, that the penny finally dropped.

Rico! It was *Rico* who'd had her investigated, not Charles. That was what that report was all about last weekend. It had nothing to do with some crooked executive at Brandon Beer. Rico had been delivering the evidence against *her*.

Yet that didn't make total sense, either. If that report had been about her, why would Charles have waited till Saturday night to read it? Surely curiosity would have overtaken him to find out what was in it, post-haste.

And then the second penny dropped. He didn't have to rush to read it because he already knew what was in it. Rico had told him everything the previous night. That was why he'd come home in such a black mood, not because he'd lost at poker but because he'd found out that his wife was a cold-blooded gold-digger.

All the not-so-cold blood drained from Dominique's face as she looked back on that night from this new perspective. The things Charles had done. The things he'd made *her* do. She'd found them exciting at the time. Now she was consumed by disgust. And dismay.

A shudder ran through her as she buried her face in her hands in horror. She didn't want to think about those things. She'd thought he loved her, that his powerful needs and desires came from that love. Now she saw his actions as nothing of the kind. He'd been driven by hate, not love. And revenge. The most terrible revenge.

More things fell into place. His putting off their having a child. His probing into her past.

He must truly hate her!

Yet if that was the case, then why had he bought her that house? And let her have Rusty?

Not everything made sense. A man intent on just revenge wouldn't have done some of the really nice things he'd done this past week.

Hope filtered in beside the horror in her heart. Maybe, just maybe, his love *hadn't* turned to hate.

Maybe he'd listened to some of the surprisingly in-
tuitive things Claudia had said about her. Maybe he'd
decided in the end to give their marriage—and her—
a second chance.

Hope did spring eternal, Dominique realised as she
scrambled out of the bath and reached for a bath-
sheet. But she had to find the rest of that report and
see what else it said about her. Only then would she
know what to do, and how to act when Charles got
home.

CHAPTER TWELVE

RICO scowled at his cards. Truly, he'd had dreadful cards all night. Impossible to bluff successfully when you never got a good hand. Even so, Renée inevitably knew when he was bluffing, regardless of his cards. He wasn't sure how.

"I'm out," he said and tossed his hand down onto the table in disgust.

The sound of a tinkling "Happy Birthday" tune coming from somewhere on his person had three pairs of irritated eyes snapping towards him.

"Sorry," he said sheepishly. "That's the new ring my nephew chose for me to programme into my cellphone. He's only seven."

"We're supposed to have all phones turned off whilst we're playing," Renée reminded him tartly as Rico dived into his pocket.

"I was expecting an important call." A total lie. He'd just forgotten to turn the darned thing off. He was beginning to forget lots of things whenever he was around his nemesis these days.

"I'm out of this hand, anyway," he said as he rose, scraping back his chair. "I'll just go take this in the powder room."

No way did he want the merry widow to hear him

begging off from meeting Leanne again. She was sure to make some caustic remark about his lack of commitment with women.

Most men would think he was foolish not to take full advantage of the uncomplicated relationship which Leanne wanted with him. But Rico had found that on his second night with the blonde he'd started thinking of Renée all the more. By the time he'd said goodnight to her, he'd realised he'd much rather spend one minute in Renée's abrasive company than all the nights in the world with the likes of Leanne. He'd told her last Saturday night it was over between them but she was just the type to make a pest of herself. Spoiled, she was, and used to getting her own way with men.

"Rico," he said curtly into the phone in anticipation of the caller's identity.

"Don't let Charles know it's me on the phone," a woman's voice said abruptly. "Don't say my name."

Dominique? What in God's name was she doing ringing *him*?

"Don't worry," he ground out. "I won't."

"Can you talk freely?"

"Pretty well. I'm sitting out this hand. I came into another room to take this call so I wouldn't annoy the others. I naturally didn't think it would be you."

"Naturally. Don't worry. This conversation is going to be brief. I have just one question, Rico. Why? Why did you have me investigated?"

Rico sucked in sharply at the realisation that the

revenge Charles had been enjoying with his wife was about to come to an end. Which was all for the better in Rico's opinion. When you played with fire, you often got burnt. And Dominique was the worst kind of fire. It was way past the time that Charles got that witch out of his life, once and for all.

"I gather you found the report," he said drily. Typical, though, that she'd go snooping around as soon as Charles was out of the house. She'd probably been looking for his bank statements.

"Yes. I've read it. And listened to the tapes. *All* of them."

She sounded upset and outraged, which was no surprise. It hadn't been pleasant reading, and even less pleasant listening.

"Good," he said. "I'm glad. I never agreed with Charles not telling you up front. But trust me, he was going to. Eventually. Don't go thinking he was planning on letting bygones be bygones, because he wasn't. And don't go thinking you'll get a cent of his money because you won't succeed there, either. The game's up, Dominique. I suggest you cut your losses, take whatever expensive gifts and clothes Charles has no doubt lavished on you and run, unless you like your husband making an even bigger fool of you than you made of him for a while. Because that's what he's been doing since he found out, you know, getting his money's worth of the only wares you have worth peddling before he dumps you cold."

Her shocked gasp echoed down the line.

''That hurt, did it?'' Rico snarled. ''Good. Because you should have been there when I told Charles the truth about you last Friday night. I'd never seen such hurt before in my life. The man was shattered.''

''Oh, God. Oh, poor Charles. But you...you're wrong about me, Rico. And I think you're wrong about Charles. I have no doubt he *was* hurt by this report and I could never explain how much I regret that. He might even have wanted revenge to begin with, but I think he changed his mind about me this past week. He saw that I really did love him. He understood where I was coming from when I was the person in that report. He bought us a house, did you know that? A house to raise a family in. Does a man planning on dumping his wife do that?''

Rico was momentarily taken aback by this news. Charles hadn't said a word to him about a house. There again, they hadn't had an opportunity to talk this past week. He'd been flat out filming the next few episodes of *A Passion for Pasta*. Then tonight, he'd deliberately cut the timing fine so that he arrived at the presidential suite right on the dot of eight and didn't have time to engage in any idle chit-chat before the game started. Repartee with Renée pre-cards was always a hazardous activity.

Still, if Charles had changed his mind about Dominique's character, surely he would have rung him and told him so. No, she was just grasping at straws.

''Are you quite sure of that?'' he threw back at

her. "It's very easy to put a deposit on a home, you know. Quite another thing to go through with the sale and exchange contracts. He's just stringing you along, honey, keeping you sweet for a while longer. Trust me when I tell you there will be no house and no family for you. Not with Charles."

"I...I don't believe you," she said, though she sounded shaken. "Charles would never do something as vile as that."

"Really? Why don't you ask him when he gets home tonight?"

"I...I won't be here."

"Excellent idea."

"No doubt you think so. Charles might not. But everything's ruined now. I can see that. Our marriage might have worked if you hadn't been around."

"You mean if my cousin, Claudia, hadn't been your flatmate."

"Your *cousin*! Oh, oh, I see. Yes, I see."

"I doubt it. Women like you see nothing but your own selfish agendas. You don't see the human wreckage you leave behind. All men are just suckers in your eyes."

"Charles said you were going through a cynical phase, but he was wrong," she said. "You're warped. Totally warped. I love Charles and I'm never going to say differently. It's you who's hurt him, Rico. You're the one who's shattered his life. He could have been happy with me. We could have been happy. And now it's all been ruined."

"You don't honestly expect me to believe that crap, do you? You *never* loved him."

"You're wrong. I did. I do. I always will. Falling for him came as a surprise, that's true. I *had* targeted him as a candidate to marry for money but all that changed the moment I met the man."

"Bullshit. You and I both know that if Charles had been some ordinary guy working for a wage, you'd never have married him."

"If Charles had been some ordinary guy I wouldn't have fallen in love with him in the first place."

"Oh, right. That's convenient logic for you. And one I've heard before, how it's easier to love a rich man than a poor man," he sneered.

Her sigh sounded weary. "I know I'll never convince you. I'm not really trying to. You've won, anyway. My marriage is over. I can't stay with Charles now because he'll never really believe in my love. There will always be that part of him which doubts. I couldn't bear that. I'll leave Charles a note saying why I've gone. And I'll tell him to go ahead with a divorce. You don't have to mention this call or the rotten things you said about him. I won't. But he'll need a good friend after I'm gone. Maybe you could be that for once instead of such a narrow-minded, cynical, self-centred bastard. Goodbye, Rico. Good luck. You're going to need it."

She slammed her phone down, leaving Rico without the opportunity of a final word. Frustrating, that.

Angrily, he switched the cellphone right off then

headed back to the card table, telling himself that it was good riddance to bad rubbish. The wormy feelings wriggling around in his stomach had nothing to do with guilt. He was hungry, that was all.

"Time for supper, isn't it?" he said to the others on his return. They'd obviously finished the hand with Charles gathering the pot over to his side and flashing him a happy smile.

Rico's stomach churned some more.

"Who was it on the phone?" Charles asked.

Rico opened his mouth, then closed it again.

"A female, no doubt," Renée said drily.

"Leanne, was it?" Charles tried.

"No."

"And who's Leanne?" Renée asked.

"Some blonde Rico's been seeing," Charles supplied, which raised Renée's finely plucked brows.

"Really? That's surprising. I thought only gentlemen preferred blondes."

"I'm stopping this before it starts," Ali said firmly. "Back to cards. Supper will be at ten-thirty as it always is, Rico. Now *deal*."

He dealt, but the call from Dominique remained at the forefront of his mind, and his revolving stomach did not settle. He kept wondering if he could possibly have been wrong where Charles's wife was concerned. What if she *had* loved him? What if Charles had discovered that for himself this past week and decided against a divorce? This would better explain his buying her a house rather than the cruel and callous motive *he'd* attributed to that move.

Charles would never be that cruel or callous. It wasn't in his nature...

Rico looked across the table and hoped like hell he hadn't just done his friend the most appalling disservice.

CHAPTER THIRTEEN

CHARLES had never seen Rico play worse. Something was on his mind. That phone call. Had he been lying when he'd said it wasn't from Leanne?

Possibly.

When supper came, he pulled Rico slightly to one side. "All right, I want the truth now. That call was from Leanne, wasn't it? You just didn't want Renée to know."

"No. It wasn't from Leanne," Rico repeated, his body language betraying agitation.

"Then who? Come on. Out with it!"

"Did you or did you not buy a house this week?" came his surprising words.

Charles blinked. Good lord! Who *was* that on the phone? The real-estate agent?

"Have you decided *not* to divorce Dominique?" Rico swept on. "*You* give it to *me* straight."

Charles was glad to. He'd only been waiting for the right opportunity. "No. I'm not going to divorce Dominique, and yes, I have bought us a house."

Rico's uncensored expletives had Renée's head snapping round from where she was still sitting at the card table, sipping her coffee.

"What is it?" she asked, sounding concerned. "What's happened?"

"Nothing," Charles returned brusquely. "Just a personal matter between us boys."

"You mean it's about women and sex," she muttered in a caustic tone.

"No, it bloody well isn't!" Charles countered. He too was growing tired of Renée's sarcasm. "It's about women and love. We men do know the difference, you know. And we occasionally embrace the latter."

She flushed whilst Rico groaned. Charles didn't like the sound of that groan. It carried far too much guilt.

"I'm beginning to get worried, Rico," he growled in low tones. "I think you should tell me what this is all about and stop playing word games. Who was that on the phone and what did they want?"

Rico looked stricken and Charles began to panic.

"It was Dominique," Rico blurted out. "She...she found the report."

Charles's expletives surpassed Rico's. He grabbed Rico's arm and shook him. "Tell me what she said!"

"She said she won't be there when you get home. She said she wants a divorce."

Charles imagined there'd been a lot more said than that. Rico's obvious remorse spelled out a far more lengthy and volatile exchange than that. But he didn't have time to find out the details right now.

Charles whirled to face his host, who was staring at him from across the room. Charles appreciated that his uncharacteristic swearing just now would have shocked Ali, who was such a gentleman. "I have to go, Ali. And I have to go *now*."

He was already off and sprinting for the door before he'd uttered that last shouted word. The ride down in the lift was sheer torment but he ran again once the lift doors whooshed open on the ground floor. He didn't stop for the parking valet to collect his car. That would take too much time. He bolted down the ramp and out onto the city street, racing for home.

He made the apartment block in three minutes flat, the security guard in the foyer looking startled as he charged in.

"Have you seen my wife tonight, Jim?" he demanded to know as his chest heaved.

The man frowned. "No, Mr Brandon. I haven't. But my shift only started at ten. Is there something wrong? Anything I can do?"

"No. No, nothing you can do," Charles muttered and hurried over to the lift well.

One minute later he was letting himself into the penthouse and feeling as if he was going to be sick. The place had some lights on but it sounded quiet. *Too* quiet.

Charles was almost afraid to go further in. He didn't want to find out what he already suspected. He was too late. She was gone.

The sudden appearance of Rusty curling around his

feet brought a surge of desperate hope. Surely she wouldn't have left her beloved cat behind?

"Dominique?" he called out, appalled at how frightened he sounded. But that was the truth of it. He was terrified that he'd lost her. No, *more* than terrified. His soul was screaming inside.

Bending to pick up the cat, he held her tight as he made his way reluctantly down to the bedroom. That would be the first sign. If her clothes were still there, then so would she be.

They were there.

Charles almost cried with relief. Now he hurried back to the living area, calling her name as he went.

But the living room was empty, as was the kitchen, the terrace. Everywhere. Maybe she'd just gone out for a walk, or possibly to a hotel for the night as a kind of protest. She'd be back soon, or in the morning. No way would she leave Rusty behind permanently.

For the first time since he'd entered the penthouse, his heartbeat slowed a little from its frantic pace and he began to have some real hope. Lowering the cat gently onto her favourite chair, Charles turned on the television then hurried to check his study and the guest suite to make sure Dominique wasn't in any of those rooms.

The letter was in the study, on his desk, weighed down by the black jewelry box he'd bought for her the previous Friday night. Charles approached both objects with the dread of certainty in his heart. He *was* too late. She *was* gone.

He lowered himself onto his chair in something of a daze, shock now taking over. His hands shook as he slid the two handwritten pages from under the box and began to read.

My darling Charles.

I do hope you don't mind my calling you that because that is what you will always be to me. My darling Charles. First, let me explain how I came to find that report. I didn't pry into your desk, if that's what you're thinking. I wanted some music to listen to whilst I was having my bubble bath and borrowed your portable player from your study. I pressed the wrong play button without even realising that there was a tape already in it or that it even played tapes…

Charles groaned. The tape! He'd left the damned thing in there. God, what a stupid thing to do!

…Naturally, once I heard what was on that tape I put two and two together and realised the report Rico had given you last Saturday had been about me, although when I thought about it some more, I guessed he'd already told you what was in it the night before.

Charles, first let me say how sorry I am that my past behaviour hurt you as much as it obviously did. I can only imagine how upset you must have been at the time. So I don't condemn you for what you thought of me and what you did that night, or during this past week. I understand how pain makes people do things they wouldn't normally do. I wasn't going to mention this but I rang Rico tonight when you were playing cards because I wanted to find out why he had me investigated. I was a tad upset myself at the time. Anyway, when Rico suggested that your buying the house might have been a part of some kind of revenge and that you probably never meant to go through with the sale, I have to confess I felt sick for a moment...

"Oh, no," Charles groaned, hating for her to think that.

But in the end, I chose not to believe Rico's idea. I chose to believe you'd already discovered you still loved me as I loved you. Of course, that doesn't mean that your love for me can possibly survive. It can't. Of course it can't. And I am entirely to blame. I took a path in life which was as warped and twisted as the path Rico is currently taking. People who act like he does—and how I did for years—have their own private hells. You brought me out of my hell, my darling. You restored my faith in the human race. You even made me see that money—or the lack of it—is not what brings happiness or unhappiness.

It is so easy to condemn others for what they do, especially when there is no sympathy or understanding. Rico has lost the capacity for sympathy and understanding. I actually feel sorry for him and hope that one day he meets a woman who will truly love him for himself. I just hope he believes her when she comes along.

But time is hurrying by and I really want to get going. I don't want to still be here when you get home. I don't want you persuading me to stay when I know I should go.

I am leaving you Rusty for two reasons. To show you that I believe you don't hate me. Not down deep, in your heart. And secondly because I don't think it's fair on Rusty to give her another change of home. She likes it there. Keep her, Charles, as a memento of me, and when you look at her, think only of how much I truly loved you. It was never a question of money. Even I can see that now. It was always a question of love.

I've left behind all the clothes and things you bought me because to take them would be to prove Rico right. Thankfully, I still have my own car and some savings. I will be in touch after a period of time so that you will know where to send the divorce papers. Needless to say I also don't want anything in the way of alimony, so please don't go making any generous gestures. I'll just give it all away. See? I've grown up at long last.

I must go. I've already stayed too long.

Don't be too hard on Rico. He probably thought
he had your best interests at heart. All my love,
                                        Dominique.

Charles slumped back in his chair, the pages resting
limply in his lap. What was he going to do? What
could he do?

He leant forward and opened the black box and
there lay the necklace in all its corrupting glory. But
it wasn't the necklace which moved him to tears. It
was the sight of his wife's wedding and engagement
rings resting with the circle of gold and opals.

There was something awfully final—and heart-
wrenching—about a woman leaving her rings behind.

The doorbell ringing jolted him out of any self-pity
and sent him racing to answer. She'd come back.
She'd changed her mind and come back!

"Dominique!" he cried out as he wrenched open
the door.

It wasn't Dominique. It was Rico, standing there
looking as bleak as Charles was suddenly feeling
again.

"Oh," Charles said flatly. "It's only you."

Rico visibly winced. "I remembered Dominique
said you'd need a friend. So I came straight away."

Charles laughed, its hollow, brittle sound echoing
in the marble-tiled foyer. "I think you've been a
friend too much already, don't you?"

"I'm sorry, Charles. I really thought she was bad

for you. You have to agree the evidence looked damning.''

Charles sighed. Rico was right. That report had been damning. ''She left me a letter,'' he said wearily. ''Maybe you should read it.''

Rico glanced up after he'd finished, his eyes sad. ''She sounds so different from what I always imagined.''

''She was.''

''I think she really loved you.''

''I *know* she really loved me.''

Saying it out loud gave Charles a spurt of much needed energy, and resolve. ''I'm going to go after her and get her back.''

''Good idea,'' Rico agreed. ''But where do you think she's gone?''

''Probably to some city hotel for the night to begin with. We'll start ringing around.''

They rang every hotel but no one by the name of Dominique Brandon had booked in.

''Maybe she's using a different name,'' Rico suggested.

''And maybe she's not in Sydney at all,'' Charles returned thoughtfully. ''Maybe she's driven well away from here.''

''To where?''

''I don't know. I'll have to think. She would have a plan. Dominique would always have a plan.''

''I think her first priority was to just get well away

from here, Charles. And you. Given the size of Australia, she could be anywhere.''

''I might have to hire that detective again to find her. The one you hired for that report.''

''Do you honestly think that's a good idea?''

''Yes. I have to find her, Rico.''

Rico sighed. ''I don't think she's going to be happy with your hiring some PI to track her down. I think you should wait till she gets in touch. She said she would. She needs time, Charles.''

Charles groaned. Maybe Rico was right. But maybe he was wrong.

''I'm so sorry, Charles,'' Rico apologised again. ''I didn't mean to hurt you like this.''

Charles patted Rico's arm. ''It's all right. You meant well, but perhaps you shouldn't be so hasty to judge people in future. Look, I'll do what you suggest and wait a little while. But no more than a month. If I haven't heard from her by then, I'm going to go and find her myself!''

CHAPTER FOURTEEN

THE day was bitter, the watery sun providing no warmth at all. But the west side of Tasmania was like that in the winter. Dominique buttoned up her overcoat, then opened the back door of her car and lifted out the flowers she'd brought with her. Yellow roses, they were. Her mother's favourite flower.

She trudged over the spongy earth, trying not to look at the tumbled-down headstones. But it was hard not to notice the general state of neglect in Keats Ridge cemetery. Still, it was no different from the town itself, which was even more run-down than she remembered.

She headed straight for the spot where she knew the grave was located, fearful now that her mother's resting place might not even *have* a headstone. She hadn't been back here in ten years and had no idea what her father had done after she'd left.

No idea what he'd done where her mother's grave was concerned that was, she thought bitterly. She knew what else he'd done. He'd gone and got himself a decent job, then a new wife who'd given him two new sons whom he obviously supported very well. That was what he'd done.

Dominique was still struggling to understand that

part of the report. Why hadn't her father been able to do that for her mother, and for her? Why had he left them both to cope alone whilst he'd drunk what little money there was?

Whatever the reason, it would have to remain a mystery. Because no way was she going to look him up and ask what miracle had caused this massive turn-around, despite the mining town he now lived in being less than an hour's drive away. She just wouldn't know what to say to him. She'd hated him too long to trust herself to even be polite. No, there was no point in fronting up there, just out of curiosity. She was going to go straight back to the mainland today, where she might have the courage to ring Charles and find out how *he* was coping.

Just on a month it had been since she'd left him. It felt like an eternity. She'd spent most of the time in a guest house in a small seaside village to the west of Melbourne, a place she'd visited once and found peaceful.

But there was no peace for the wicked and Dominique had found her days and nights plagued with never-ending feelings of remorse and regret. Reading that report and hearing Rico say how much it had hurt Charles had really brought home to her how unconscionably she'd acted in the decade since her mother's death. She'd used people, perhaps not callously, but selfishly and insensitively. And she'd had only one goal. Money.

As much as she would have liked to wallow in self-pity that her marriage to Charles had failed, she could find none. She'd been as guilty as hell of the gold-digger tag Rico had given her. There were no excuses, really, only reasons. And the main reason lay here, in this cemetery, in…

Surprise ground Dominique to a halt. Because before her lay not what she'd feared. Not a ramshackle mound with grass and weeds growing over it and a cheap cross marking the site, but a beautifully kept grave covered by a full marble slab in a lovely grey colour with a large matching headstone.

The simple words carved into it touched Dominique deeply.

Tess Cooper, beloved wife of Scott Cooper, beloved mother of Jane Cooper. A beautiful woman. May she truly rest in peace.

She sank down onto her knees beside the grave, her hand reaching out to touch her mother's name. Guilt flooded in over the reality that this was the first time she'd visited here since the funeral. Ten years ago today her mother had been buried. Ten *years*, and she hadn't been back. Not once.

''Oh, Mum,'' she cried softly. ''Forgive me…''

Yet someone had visited not that long back. There were some dried-up flowers in the built-in vase, which indicated someone had come here not all that long ago.

''Forgive me,'' she choked out again, tears flooding her eyes as she took the dead flowers out and replaced them with her own.

"I hoped and prayed I'd find you here today."

Dominique gasped and jumped to her feet, spinning round at the same time.

"Charles!" she exclaimed, lifting her hands to dash away her tears and focus on the man she loved. Dear God, he looked thin. And tired. And every one of his forty years. "But how—?"

"Don't ask," he interrupted, his voice thick with emotion. "And don't argue. Just come home.

"Come home," he repeated when she just stood there, stunned. He'd come all this way after her. He must really love her if he still wanted her back, even now.

"But…"

"There are no buts," he ground out. "When I married you I married you for better or worse, for richer or poorer, in sickness and in health till death us do part. That report was the worse but I am not going to divorce you, Dominique. I love you. I will always love you, no matter what. If you truly love me then you will come home with me. Today. Because I cannot bear another day without you. And neither can Rusty. We're both pining for you, my darling. We need you. Come home with me. But first…just come here." And he reached out to her.

She burst into tears then fell into his arms.

He gathered her in close and hugged her till she didn't have enough breath to keep crying.

"No more tears now," he ordered. "We're going to go home together and be happy in our happy house. Yes, I really did buy the place. I always meant to. Rico has been mortified over what he implied about that. There was no revenge in my heart after that first night, Dominique. That's the honest to God truth. The contracts were exchanged on the house last week and I've already moved the furniture in from the penthouse, which actually looks quite good. Rusty was ecstatic to be back in her own home, till she discovered you weren't there. Then she went off her food again."

Dominique pulled back to gaze up into her husband's drawn face. "You look like you've been off your food too, Charles."

He smiled. "I need you to cook for me."

"Who's looking after Rusty whilst you're down here?"

"Rico volunteered for the job. Poor man. Renée's not speaking to him at all now. She blames him for breaking up our marriage. Friday nights at poker have been very quiet, I can tell you. And a tad boring. I didn't realise how entertaining Rico and Renée's spats were till they stopped. But then..."

"Jane? *Jane?* Is that you?"

Dominique whirled in Charles's arms, sinking back against him once her eyes confirmed what her ears had already told her.

"It *is* you?" her father said. "Good God, I'd forgotten just how much like Tess you were."

Dominique stood there, staring at the man before her. He looked good. No, be honest, damn you. He looked great, despite his greying hair and a few added pounds. There again, he wasn't all that old. He'd only been eighteen when she was born. Which made him…what? Forty-six. Not much older than Charles.

She stared first at his face, then at the bouquet of yellow roses he was holding.

"It was you, then, who's been visiting here?" she asked, disbelief in her voice.

He nodded and came forward to put his roses in with hers. They made quite a show.

"I come every couple of months or so," he said. "Make sure everything's kept nice for her. You know how she liked everything to be nice."

Dominique remembered. So particular her mother was, with her person, and her home. Too bad that home had only been a shack.

"How can you bear to come here?" Dominique blurted out. "Today of all days! How can you face her after what you did?"

She felt Charles's hands tighten on her upper arms. "Remember what you said in your letter," her husband told her gently, "about there always being reasons for people doing the things they do. Give the man a hearing, darling. He deserves that, at least."

"Thank you," her father said. "I appreciate that. And you are?"

"The name is Charles Brandon. I'm Dominique's husband."

"Dominique? But…"

"I changed my name after I left here," Dominique said sharply, and her father nodded. Slowly. Sadly.

"I understand. You wanted to forget. I don't blame you. I wanted to forget, too."

"You seemed to have managed that quite well," she threw at him. "A new wife. Two new sons."

"You know about them?" He was very taken aback.

"I know everything. I know all about your wonderful new job as well. So tell me, Dad, how did you manage all that, given that when I left here the day of Mum's funeral you were nothing but a pathetic drunk with no pride and no guts?"

"For pity's sake, Dominique," Charles said with a groan.

"No," her father said. "She has every right to feel the way she does. I had become exactly what she said. A pathetic drunk. I couldn't cope with her mother's illness, or her fears. I should never have promised her what I promised her in the first place. It was weak of me, but then I was always weak where Tess was concerned. I loved her too much to go against her wishes, especially after I'd lost my job. I felt…powerless. Useless. Drinking was the easy way out and I took it. I took it and I left it to my teenage daughter to carry the load which should have been mine."

"You're not making any sense," Dominique snapped, having no patience with him at all. "What wishes are you talking about? What fears? Mum was very brave when she was dying. Much braver than I could ever be. And much, much braver than you!''

"Yes, she was brave. But it was a bravery that was so unnecessary.''

"You can say that again. If only you'd taken her to some decent doctors, she might not have died at all.''

"You think I didn't want that? I begged her and begged her to get medical help but she refused. She wouldn't go to doctors. Not after her experience when she was having you.''

"What kind of experience?''

"She said the doctor who looked after her during her pregnancy touched her in not a nice way whenever he was examining her. She didn't tell me about it till after you were born. When she did she cried and cried for days. After that, she began to be afraid of lots of things. The city. Crowds. Most men. We went to live in Keats Ridge because it was so remote. Unfortunately, some of her fears came with her. Her fear of men, and doctors. Yet the doctor there was a very good man. You knew him, Jane. Dr Wilson. Tess would take you to him but she never went to him herself. Not once. When she kept miscarrying I begged her to go and see him and have one of those pap smear tests but she refused. She said she'd get better all by herself and she did for a while, although she never did fall pregnant again. Around the time I lost my job she got a lump in her breast. She said it couldn't be cancer because it didn't hurt. But she wasn't well. Then eventually, the pain started. I think the cancer had gotten into her bones by then. Finally, it went to her lungs and that was the beginning of the end.''

Dominique could hardly believe what she was hearing. ''But Mum told me she *had* gone to the doctor. She told me he said there was nothing they could do, it was too late to operate. When I asked her why you didn't take her down to the hospital in Hobart and see a cancer specialist for a second opinion, she said you said we couldn't afford it.''

Her father's face reflected true horror. ''But that's not true! I would have taken her in a flash. And it wouldn't have cost a thing, since I was unemployed. She just wouldn't go. She wouldn't even leave the town so that I could find work. Her fear of the outside world and doctors was greater than her fear of death, I tell you.''

''But that's crazy!''

''Yes, I know. It was. And it almost drove *me* crazy, watching her die like that. But you don't know what she was like when you weren't around, the way she would beg me to stay here and not do anything. In the end, I was beyond doing much, anyway, as you well know. I did get some morphine tablets for her, which gave her some relief from the pain. After she died and you left, I took all the rest of the tablets and almost died myself. But I didn't. Doc Wilson saved me then brought in a social worker for some coun-selling, as they do in all attempted suicides. She was very kind. Very…understanding. Her name was Karen and she helped me get my life back on track. I moved over to Holt Mountain, went to AA, got myself a job and two years after Tess died Karen and I were married.''

Dominique didn't know what to say. As much as her father's story had answered a lot of questions, she still could not put aside the hatred she'd lived on for most of her life. ''How nice for you,'' she bit out.

His eyes looked terribly sad and she began to hate herself.

''I'm sorry, Jane. Sorry I let your mother down. But especially sorry I let *you* down. It's troubled me a lot these past ten years, thinking of how angry and bitter you were at your mother's funeral and knowing how much you despised me. I see now you must have thought I was entirely to blame; that I could have saved Tess if only I'd been stronger and taken her down to Hobart and made her see a doctor. And you're right. That's exactly what I should have done. But I didn't and I can't go back. What's done is done. All I can do for Tess now is come here and make sure her grave is as she would have liked it to be.''

When he took a step towards her, she shrank back into Charles, her face warning him to keep his distance.

He shook his head slowly in an attitude of defeat. ''I can't tell you how many times I've hoped to find you here. Just seeing you here today, seeing that you're alive and well…'' His throat convulsed. His hands balled into fists at his sides. "It…it means a lot to me, Jane. I have worried about you so much, although I dare say you don't believe me. I wasn't much of a father. But if you could find it in your heart to forgive me, I…I…"

He broke off, his shoulders shaking as his eyes dropped to the ground. "Oh, God," he sobbed.

How she found herself in his arms was a mystery and a miracle. Had Charles propelled her there or had she gone herself, driven by the need to forgive her father so that she could forgive herself for all the things *she'd* done during her life, and deeply regretted?

"It's all right, Daddy," she cried, hugging him close and sharing his very true pain. For both of them had a lot to feel remorseful over. "I do forgive you. I *do*. It's all right. It's all right."

Charles watched them with tears in his own eyes. But his tears were tears of relief, not distress. Because Dominique's emotional refrain carried the ring of truth. It *was* going to be all right. For her father. For her. And for him.

Wonderfully, incredibly all right.

CHAPTER FIFTEEN

"I...I FEEL nervous," Dominique said as Charles angled her silver car into their new driveway at Clifton Gardens.

It had taken them three days to make it home from Tasmania. One getting back to the mainland by boat from Devonport, then two days driving from Melbourne to Sydney with a stop over in a motel outside of Goulburn.

"Nervous about what?" Charles asked after parking next to Rico's fiery red Ferrari.

"About facing Rico."

"There's nothing for you to be nervous about. He was thrilled about our being back together again when I rang him the other night."

They both climbed out of the car and walked together up the front path.

Dominique sighed as she mounted the front porch. "Somehow I find that hard to believe."

The man himself wrenched open the front door before Charles could produce a key.

"And about time too," he grumped. "I could have driven to Timbuktu and back in the time it's taken you two to get home."

"Dominique doesn't like me driving her car too fast," Charles explained.

"What? Oh, yes, you flew down there, didn't you? And rented a car. Hi there, Dominique. You're looking extra well. Am I glad you've patched things up with Hubbie here. You've no idea how impossible he's been without you. Your cat's been just as bad. At least she *was* till this morning, when she suddenly decided to stop whining and eat. Must have known you were coming home. Anyway, she's asleep in front of the television after devouring two tins of that super-duper spoiled-kitty-cat food Charles bought for her. Look, sorry to cut and run but I'm way behind in my filming schedule for this week, as you can imagine. See you tomorrow night at poker, Charles. And don't forget, I will expect a dinner invite soon to make up for all I have endured this past month or so. But don't serve pasta, Dominique. I'm sick to death of the stuff. *Ciao!*"

Sweeping up an overnight bag he had at the ready, Rico was gone before Dominique could say boo, the tyres on his Ferrari screeching a little as he backed out, then zoomed up the street.

"Goodness!" she exclaimed. "Is he often like that?"

"Only when *he* feels nervous," Charles said with a wry smile. "But don't worry. He'll be back to being his normal obnoxious self in no time."

"I dare say. But I'll still invite him to dinner. Maybe he can bring Renée with him."

Charles laughed. "Over Renée's dead body."

"She *really* doesn't like Rico?"

Charles pondered that question, trying to see if there might be some unwanted attraction behind Renée's hostility. "I'm not sure," he said in the end. "Look, I'll extend an invite to them both tomorrow night and see what happens, shall I?"

"Yes. Yes, do that, Charles."

"I'd better go and bring in our cases."

"No, don't do that yet. Take me for a tour first and let me see what you've been doing with my house."

"Not much, I can assure you. I just filled up the cupboards in the kitchen and had the penthouse furniture brought over."

Dominique walked down the central hallway into the kitchen and then the family room, letting the atmosphere she'd first felt in the place wash through her. Rusty woke as she passed and jumped down from the lounge chair to follow her, curling around Dominique's legs when she finally stopped in the master bedroom.

Smiling, she bent down to pick her up. "I was right, Rusty, wasn't I?" she murmured as she placed the cat on the bed and stroked her ears. "It *is* a happy house."

"It will be now that you're in it," Charles said, and Dominique turned to him, her eyes glistening.

"What a lovely thing to say. But then…you're a lovely man. How can I ever begin to thank you for coming after me? And for loving me, despite everything? I...I don't deserve it."

"Yes, you do. You deserve the very best and I aim to make sure you always have it. You had a rotten time of it as a kid, Dominique. I do understand what made your father act the way he did, but I can't condone it. He can't, either. It was generous of you to forgive him. *Very* generous."

"How could I not when you forgave me?" she choked out. "Besides, he wasn't always a bad father. I'd forgotten how good he was in my younger years, when he had a job, and before Mum got sick. People have a tendency to forget the good bits and only remember the bad."

"That's true."

"I wish I'd understood my mother more. I wish she'd confided in me instead of letting me think the things I thought."

"She couldn't, Dominique. She would have been too afraid to tell you the truth. She would have been worried about losing your love, and your respect."

"Yes, yes, I can see that now. I just wish that... Oh, I don't know what I wish."

"Your father said it all, Dominique. You can't go back. He can't go back. What's done is done. All we can do is learn from our mistakes and forge a better future than our pasts."

"Promise me you'll always tell me the truth," she said, her voice catching. "Promise me."

"I promise."

"Me too." Dominique swallowed. "What…what did you do with my rings?"

"They're here, waiting for you." Drawing them out of his jacket pocket, he came forward and slipped them back onto her left hand.

"For better or worse, Dominique," he said, lifting her hand to his lips. "For richer or poorer. In sickness and in health… Forever and ever."

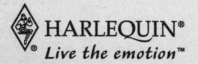